Tug of War

JOAN LINGARD

PUFFIN BOOKS

PUFFIN BOOKS
Published by the Penguin Group
Penguin Books USA Inc., 375 Hudson Street, New York, New York 10014, U.S.A.
Penguin Books Ltd, 27 Wrights Lane, London W8 5TZ, England
Penguin Books Australia Ltd, Ringwood, Victoria, Australia
Penguin Books Canada Ltd, 10 Alcorn Avenue, Toronto, Ontario, Canada M4V 3B2
Penguin Books (N.Z.) Ltd, 182–190 Wairau Road, Auckland 10, New Zealand

Penguin Books Ltd, Registered Offices: Harmondsworth, Middlesex, England

First published in Great Britain by Hamish Hamilton Children's Books, 1989
First published in the United States of America by Lodestar Books, an affiliate of Dutton Children's Books, a division of Penguin Books, USA Inc., 1990
Published in Puffin Books, 1992
1 3 5 7 9 10 8 6 4 2

LIBRARY OF CONGRESS CATALOGING-IN-PUBLICATION DATA
Lingard, Joan.
Tug of war / by Joan Lingard. p. cm.
Summary: Follows the ordeal of fourteen-year-old twins Astra and Hugo Petersons, as they and their family flee their native Latvia before the advancing Russian armies in late 1944 and find themselves homeless refugees in a war-torn Germany.
ISBN 0-14-036072-7
1. World War, 1939–1945—Latvia—Juvenile fiction. [1. World War, 1939–1945—Latvia—Fiction. 2. Refugees—Fiction. 3. World War, 1939–1945—Germany—Fiction.] I. Title.
PZ7.L6626Tu 1992 [Fic]—dc20 92-5129

Printed in the United States of America
Set in Meridien

for the Birkhans family
in Scotland, Canada, and Latvia

N
W
E
S
NORWAY
NORTH
SEA
DENMARK
Cuxhaven
Kiel
HOLLAND
Bremen
Hamburg
Lüneburg
Stettin
Hanover
BELGIUM
GERMANY
Cologne
Leipzig
Gera
Frankfurt
Rhine River
Stuttgart
PRAGUE
FRANCE
Esslingen
Munich
SWITZERLAND
VIENNA
AUSTRIA
ITALY

ALTIC SEA
ESTONIA
Leningrad
Cesis
Riga
LATVIA
Liepaja
LITHUANIA
Gdynia
Danzig
EAST
PRUSSIA
RUSSIA
Poznań
WARSAW
Lodz
POLAND
LEGEND
The route followed by the Petersons
across Europe during World War II
0
100
200
Miles
LOVAKIA
BUDAPEST
HUNGARY
ROMANIA

Tug of War

1

"THIRTY MINUTES," said Lukas Petersons. "And then we must go. The train will not wait. Fetch your bags, children! We should have gone before—last month, or even earlier," he added in a quiet aside to his wife, Kristina, who was standing behind him, hands clenched tightly in front of her.

Astra heard the aside. She heard, too, her mother say, "It'll be all right, Lukas, as long as we get the train. . . ."

Hugo and Tomas had already gone upstairs. Astra slipped out onto the verandah. The old rocking chair was still sitting there with its patchwork cushion faded from sun and air, her tennis racket stood propped up in the corner looking scuffed around the edges, a pair of Tomas's canvas sandals lay underneath the rattan table on which they breakfasted on sunny summer mornings. Had breakfasted. They were unlikely to again. Unless—no, they had given up expecting miracles. It was largely through hoping for them that they had waited so long.

She dropped down into the rocking chair and rocked a little, keeping one foot on the floor, letting her head rest against the raffia back. It was their fourteenth birthday—

hers and Hugo's. The twenty-fourth of September, 1944. They'd got up before dawn and walked together through the fields. They'd seen the sun rise. Where shall we be this time next year, they had asked each other. They'd watched a formation of ducks grouping overhead, then wheeling away southward. Emigrating, Hugo had said, like them. Except that they knew that they might not return in the spring with the birds.

Astra continued to rock. An unusual torpor had come over her at the very moment when they must gather themselves together and flee. I could sit here forever, she thought. On the lawn in front of the house two fat blackbirds were waddling up and down, stopping to dip their heads and peck at the grass. In the distance the sound of artillery fire rumbled on.

It had been a good summer, in spite of the constant noise of the war going on in the distance. Odd, perhaps, that it should have been, but it was. They had helped on Klavins' farm, all three of them, even Tomas, who had herded cows in his bare feet, walking in the cow pats to warm them in early morning, and they had swum in the river on lazy, still evenings, watching the dragonflies skimming the surface of the green water. And she had walked through the meadows with Klavins' son Valdis, their feet cutting swathes through the clover and buttercups. He had taken her hand and they had swung their arms loosely between them. Hugo had been fed up. "Don't be jealous," she had told him. She wanted to smile when she remembered the look on Hugo's face, but instead found that hot tears were pricking her eyes. She blinked to chase them away. When she thought of Valdis her throat felt thick, as if she had a cold coming. After today she might never see him again.... Of course she would see him! They were leaving for only a little while, until this horrible war could be sorted out.

For months everyone had been talking about the advance of the Russian army into the Baltic states. But until they had actually heard the whine of aircraft and the crackle of gunfire and watched the night sky exploding into flame, they had not quite been able to believe that one day it would arrive *here,* in this place which was their home. It was such a peaceful spot, deep in the countryside. They had lulled themselves into thinking that they might be able to lie low, since they were so tucked away, with woods all around, protecting them, keeping them safe. They ought to have known that no one is safe in war.

And now the Russians were in Estonia to the north and Lithuania to the south and in possession of part of eastern and central Latvia, which meant that the country was split in two. Their father had shown them on the map the evening before. Their only escape route was a narrow strip beside the Baltic Sea running down the Courland peninsula. Apart from that, they were boxed in. And from there the only way out of the country would be by sea. To Germany. There was nowhere else to go. Earlier in the war some of their friends had slipped away in boats under cover of darkness to Sweden. They should have followed their friends' example, but it was too late now—small boats could no longer slide undetected into the darkness.

Stay and live under Russian occupation, or go to Germany—these were the choices they had. For their father the first option would be suicidal; he was on a list of those classified as Enemies of the People by the Russians, who would almost certainly deport him to Siberia. He was an educated man, a classical scholar, and a university professor, and he owned land, not a great deal, but enough to be listed. Enemies to the Soviets meant anyone in authority or who held views opposed to communist doctrine. The categories listed included, among others, lawyers, journalists, trade union officials, hoteliers and restaurateurs, landowners, shipowners, mayors, policemen, and clergymen. When the Russians had been in occupation between 1940 and 1941 they had transported to Siberia more than thirty thousand men, women, and children. Most had gone during one night of terror when people had cowered in darkness, listening to the ring of sharp booted heels on the pavement, waiting for a knock on the door.

Their father had spent that year in hiding. He could not hope to do it again and survive. They'd lived in the capital, Riga, then. Lukas's younger brother, Gunnars, had been among those taken away by the Russians; also Astra's godfather, who was a lawyer. He'd been found later in a field, dead, with spikes driven through his head. For weeks afterward Astra had wakened gasping for breath, thinking that someone was holding her down and trying to drive spikes into *her* skull.

Lukas had gone into hiding somewhere in the city back streets; they had never known where. Best not to know, their mother had said. They had all heard the story, though, many times, until they felt they had seen it with their own eyes: of their father running and the Cheka—secret police, known to everyone as the Blue Hats—firing, and then their father doubling over with both his hands flying down to clasp his right knee, and in the next second recovering his balance and lurching on, dragging his shattered leg behind him, and then the Blue Hats firing again and their father, with a last surge, turning the corner. He had crawled away into a cellar where he'd huddled, waiting for the Blue Hats to pass and trying not to moan with the pain.

Later Lukas had managed to drag himself to the apartment of one of his friends who hid him in his loft for a few weeks. Then Paulis Jansons, the tenant at their country home, had gone into Riga with a hay cart and smuggled him out to a safe house in another part of the country. This was one of the reasons that the Jansons were going to come with them now—Paulis was on the Soviet blacklist because he'd helped Lukas Petersons.

After their father had gone into hiding, the Cheka had come to their apartment in Riga and questioned them. Their mother had been white and calm: Astra could still see her face as she'd raised it to answer the Blue Hats. They had pulled every room apart, stuck their bayonets into clothes closets and toy boxes. Astra had felt as if the tip of the bayonet were running into her own stomach.

The next day a message had come via Sils the baker: Go to the country. The family had gone and never returned to their home in the city. But Astra could never forget those men from the Cheka: the way the floors of their apartment had quivered under their heavy black boots and the sound their stamping had made. Involuntarily she put her hands over her ears.

"Astra!" her mother was calling. "What *are* you doing?"

"It's all right—I'm ready!" Astra leaped from the chair, leaving it rocking, and sprinted up the stairs to her room. Hugo's door was closed, she saw.

Hugo's packed rucksack stood just inside his bedroom door. It felt like a sack of potatoes when he tried to lift it. "You'll break your back trying to carry that!" Astra had said earlier. "You'd better take some of those books out." But he had not.

He went to the window and leaned out to take a last look. A slight wind was rippling through the birch trees, making the thin black branches tremble and the yellow-green leaves quiver. They were on the turn. In the meadow beyond he could see Klavins' black-and-white cows, all six of them, their heads down in the long grass, their tails swishing to and fro like windshield wipers. He had milked them on many occasions and had a favorite one called Milda. She would come to him and muzzle his hand and walk beside him, bumping her wide-barreled body against his.

Behind the hill at the back of the long meadow, smoke could be seen. The smoke of battle. It was not far away, no more than six miles. What if the Russians were to advance quickly, come running over the hill and across the meadow like a hot knife slicing through butter? What idiots they'd been to wait so long!

His father maintained that people nearly always did wait until the last moment and it was only then that they realized it *was* the last moment. "But I don't know why we were so reluctant to believe it," he had said. "We are used to invading armies in our country, after all." The bitterness in his voice had made them stir uneasily, for usually he spoke softly. "One goes out and another comes in. That is the history of Latvia! It is a sad fate to be a small country squeezed between two big powerful ones."

Latvia had had only twenty-two years without an army of occupation, between 1918 and 1940. When would they ever be really free, Hugo wondered, without waiting for the next army to come in? And what would it be like for them in Germany? Here, far from the city, they had seen little of the occupying German forces, but he remembered how, in July 1941, they had watched as the German troops had marched through Cesis, the nearby town, their rifles clenched to their left shoulders, their steel helmets glinting in the summer sunshine, their eyes set straight ahead.

"I hate armies," their mother had murmured.

"But they've come to free us from the Russians." Hugo had looked at her in surprise.

"I know. But they're not bringing us freedom."

When they had seen the Gestapo they had shivered, for

they had heard many tales of the brutality of the German secret police. Secret police everywhere were to be feared, their mother had said, whatever country they came from.

The Germans also purged the Latvian population, but their main targets were the Jews. They removed sixty thousand. The Russians had already deported a number, some five thousand or so. One of Lukas's closest friends, a Jew, and a professor of philosophy at the University of Riga, was taken away by the Germans along with his wife and four children. No one knew where they'd gone.

Non-Jewish university professors were left alone. So Lukas was able to come out of hiding and rejoin his family. For the last three years they had lived quietly in the country, doing nothing to attract attention. The war in Europe had continued to rage on, the Germans and Russians battling it out on Russian soil. Until early 1943 the German armies had seemed invincible, and then the tide had turned and the Russians had begun to drive the Germans back, until in March 1944 they had reached the Estonian border.

For most of that time, a German dentist, who worked at the military hospital near Cesis, had been billeted with the Petersons.' Lieutenant Schwarz was a quiet man; he liked to play chess in the evenings with his landlord and to listen to his landlady playing the piano. He did not speak of the war except when he wished that it would be over soon so that he could return home. He missed his family in Germany and would talk about them and pass their photographs around.

And now the Petersons' only hope of escaping the Russians was to go to Germany themselves. They had a contact there, an old professor of their father's from his student days in Heidelberg. Otto Zimmermann was a good, kindly man, and Hugo's godfather. Hugo was fond of him even though he had seen him only three times, when the professor had come to visit them before the war. But Professor Zimmermann had kept up a regular correspondence with both Lukas and Hugo. Now he was retired and living in Leipzig. In the spring they had had a letter from him in which he had said, "Do not hesitate to come here if the situation gets too difficult for you in Latvia. You cannot run the risk of letting yourself fall into Soviet hands, Lukas. We have a large house with plenty of room. . . ."

Last week Lukas had written to say that they were finally going to take him up on his offer.

Across the landing Astra was trying and failing to fasten the straps of her rucksack. What could she take out? She needed everything: the clothes and her toothbrush and face cloth and the talcum powder given to her by her friend Mara Jansons for her birthday, and the string of red wooden beads which had been a present from her mother and father, and the straw bag made for her by Hugo, and *Jane Eyre* written by the English novelist Charlotte Brontë and translated into Latvian. She would read it on the train. They would have to change in Riga for the Baltic port of Liepaja. It would be a long, slow journey, for everything was confused these days, with the Russians advancing and the Germans retreating and Latvians running hither and thither not sure where to go, and then there was always the risk of the trains being bombed.

By removing one of her shirts she managed to draw the strings of the sack together. She tied them firmly and fastened the buckles.

As she turned she caught sight of herself in the dressing table mirror and went closer. She sat down on the stool and leaned forward, resting her elbows on the top and her chin on her hands. This is *me,* she said to herself, Astra Petersons. She felt as if she might not see this self again. She looked into her gray eyes, raised a finger to touch the small freckles sprinkled over the bridge of her nose and across the tops of her cheeks.

It seemed to have gone very quiet everywhere. There was even a lull in the gunfire, and she could hear the sound of her own breathing in the room.

And then the artillery started up again. It had come nearer, surely?

"Wait here!" she said to the girl in the mirror, leaning forward so that her breath misted the glass. "I'll be back."

"Are you ready?" asked Hugo, who had come into the room.

Startled, Astra jumped up and whirled around, putting her back to the mirror.

At the same time their father called to them from downstairs. "Children!" His voice was becoming impatient. They could hear him walking up and down, trailing his lame leg behind him.

Hugo went first. Astra followed, after a last quick backward glance into her room. The sun was slanting in, touching the old rag rug beside her bed, lighting up its reds and blues. Her grandmother had made that rug. They had gone to say good-bye to her yesterday. She was not coming; she was too old to give up her home, she said. It had been difficult saying good-bye, and their father had wept. Their maternal grandmother was in Riga, but they would not have time to stop and see her, nor their aunt and uncle and cousins.

Astra closed the door of her room behind her and ran downstairs.

"Klavins and Valdis are here," said her father.

"A moment, Astra." Her mother beckoned to her.

Astra turned back.

Her mother held out a string of glistening yellow amber beads. "Bend your head, dear."

Astra inclined it and her mother looped the necklace over. Astra straightened up and put her hand over the beads where they lay against her throat.

"Part of the family heritage!" Kristina smiled. "I'm taking some of my amber jewelry with me, but I want you to have these now. My grandmother gave them to me on my eighteenth birthday. Wear them underneath your shirt, it might be better."

"Thank you." Astra hugged her.

Yesterday they had buried in the vegetable patch, among the potato drills, the rest of their valuables—the family silver, heavier pieces of amber, a few articles of jewelry set with precious stones, some small bronze figurines. Lukas had drawn all their savings, in German marks, from the bank some weeks before. The wad of notes was now in an oilskin pouch in the inside pocket of his overcoat.

"Take the food hamper, dear," said Kristina.

Astra lifted the wicker basket. In it she and her mother had packed rye loaves, carrot cake, potato pancakes, dried mushrooms, and a lump of hard cheese. Olga Jansons would bring milk from their cow.

The hamper pulling down her right shoulder, her rucksack slung over her left, Astra went out onto the verandah. Directly in front of it two heavy workhorses and carts were drawn up. Klavins stood by one horse, Valdis by the other. Valdis nodded at her and smiled, though she saw that he looked sad. She wished they were coming with them, but Klavins would not leave his land and his son would not leave him. Klavins said the Russians would not be interested in them; they were just poor farmers.

Lukas Petersons told his children to put their bundles into the first cart.

"Our train goes at two, Klavins."

"We should make that all right, Professor Petersons." The

farmer looked toward the horizon. "The Russians aren't far away. They'll be here in a day or two if I'm not mistaken."

As if the Russians had heard, an extra loud burst of firing started up and the horses moved restlessly. Klavins and Valdis stroked their noses and murmured a few words to calm them. Tomas put his hand up to fondle the nose of the brown-and-white horse, Feliks, which Valdis held. He was Tomas's favorite horse on the farm.

"Keep Feliks safe till I come back," he said.

"I will," said Valdis, whose eyes were still on Astra.

The leading cart was loaded up with boxes containing their household goods: dishes, pots and pans, bed linen. Each box had been clearly labeled c/o Professor Otto Zimmermann at his address in Leipzig.

Now it was time for them to climb aboard.

"Let's be off, Klavins!" said Lukas, and as they lurched down the drive and into the lane he stared resolutely ahead, not turning to look back at the house. "It's only a house," he'd said that morning. "We love it, that is true, but we must not make a fuss about leaving it. The important thing is that we shall all be together, as a family. As long as we can be together nothing else matters too much."

Although their mother did not look back, either, the three younger members of the family did; Astra and Hugo only briefly, but Tomas twisted right around and stared at the old weathered wooden house with its long verandah and apple-green door and the funny old weathercock on the rooftop. He'd forgotten to shut his window and the wind had caught hold of the white net curtain and whipped it outside where it was billowing like a sail. It looked as if it was waving good-bye. Tomas lifted his hand in salute.

"Look, Tom," said his mother, touching him on the knee, "there's Zigi!"

Zigi Jansons was standing in front of his house with his

bag between his feet, ready to go, as were the rest of his family. His mother, Olga, had baby Klara in her arms and his father, Paulis, was wearing his best Sunday-and-funeral suit which looked tight and stiff. Mara, who was Astra's friend, had her arms full of bundles. Paulis Jansons had done outdoor jobs for the Petersons while his wife had helped in the house.

The Jansons tossed their luggage on to Valdis's cart.

"Professor Petersons," said Paulis, coming to speak to Lukas, "my mother would like to come. She has decided she doesn't want to stay, after all. Would that be all right?" he asked anxiously. Yesterday Granny Jansons had been declaring that a whole team of wild horses couldn't drag her from her home.

"Of course! We would not think of leaving her behind."

"Mother!" called Paulis.

Granny Jansons came shuffling out of the house, bundled up in so many clothes and shawls that she herself was scarcely visible. She was grumbling underneath her breath, cursing both Germans and Russians alike and wishing she were dead and buried.

"Come on then, Mother," said Paulis, and with a great deal of heaving and pushing he and Mara managed to get her on board.

"We'd better get a move on!" said Lukas.

"Giddy-up!" cried Klavins and cracked his whip.

The big horses clopped on slowly, straining under their heavy loads.

Just before they reached the main road the leading cart, bearing the Petersons, skidded sideways on the muddy country lane and ended up with its back axle in the ditch.

"Everyone off!" Lukas was already sliding down from his perch. Hugo put out a hand to steady him.

Within minutes, Klavins and Valdis, helped by Hugo and Paulis, had managed to pull the cart out and right it again.

"I fear we are overloaded," said Kristina, biting her lip.

"I can walk, Father," offered Hugo.

"No, there isn't enough time. We'll miss the train. It's five miles to Cesis."

"Oh, mercy me!" cried Granny Jansons, clapping her hand to her mouth. She came sliding down off the cart to land on the road like a sack of flour. Tomas wondered that she did not burst open; she looked as if she were held together in the middle with tapes. "I've forgotten my teeth," she moaned.

"Well, we're not going back now, Mother," said her son, and putting his hands under her armpits, yanked her, protesting loudly, back onto the cart.

"I can't go without my teeth, I can't." She continued to wail and her voice mingled with the trundling of the cart wheels.

"I've never seen her with her teeth in," said Kristina softly. "But she seems to manage to eat enough."

When they emerged onto the main road the scene was such that it silenced them all. It was as if everyone in the country was on the move: men, women, and children, in carts, on bicycles, walking; soldiers on foot; gray, straggling lines of prisoners-of-war. And swerving in and out of the ragged procession, honking their horns to make people scatter and clear the way, went German armed trucks and cars. The only motorized vehicles were those belonging to the military. All private cars had been requisitioned early in the war.

"What madness!" Lukas shook his head. "Where do all these people think they're going? I suppose we had better join on and add to the chaos."

They edged into the slow-moving line of traffic, keeping well to the right, ready to shift onto the side whenever they heard a horn blaring behind them. At times they were going so slowly that the children jumped off and walked alongside.

And then they saw the plane come soaring out of the sky like a black hawk. It was a Russian twin-engined bomber. They could see the red stars on its side and wing.

"Into the ditch!" cried Lukas.

They flung themselves down, and in the next second heard the bang and felt the ground tremble. People were screaming, horses rearing and whinnying. Astra felt for Hugo's hand and Kristina threw an arm across her younger son.

"Keep down!" commanded Lukas, lifting his own head.

Another plane had appeared on the horizon, a German fighter. It came streaking toward the Russian plane, which tried to wheel about and take evasive action. They lifted their heads and watched as the two planes engaged in battle, strafing each other with bullets—the one emblazoned with the iron cross, the other with the red star. The German plane caught fire, but in the next second a ball of orange flame roared through the Russian one. Both dropped into a field a couple of miles away and a long pall of smoke rose up into the sky.

"Back into the carts," said Lukas briskly. "We have no time to stand and stare."

Dully they obeyed him. The road was strewn with bodies and farther down a huge crater had been left in the road. An army truck had stopped and some soldiers were helping the injured.

"We must get around as best we can," said Lukas. "We've got to be strong, children. We shall see plenty of things like this before we're done, I'm afraid."

They had gone only another few hundred yards when Klavins' cart slewed sideways again. This time the axle was broken. The men conferred, coming quickly to the conclusion that it could not be mended. The only thing they could do was to move all the luggage onto the other cart and let everyone walk except for Granny Jansons, Olga, and the baby.

"You cannot walk, Lukas," his wife objected.

"I shall have to."

By the time they reached the edge of the town his limp had become so bad that at times he stumbled and would have fallen had he not been held by Astra and Hugo. They walked one on either side of him, taking an arm each, paying no attention to his protests that he did not need help. Their mother's face looked pinched with worry.

"We're going to be late, aren't we, Lukas?"

"No, we should be all right." But he was frowning. "We still have fifteen minutes."

"I make it twelve," said Hugo, consulting his watch. He was meticulous about setting it to the right time every morning. Astra liked to tease him about it.

As they drew near to the station the traffic thickened. They rounded the last corner and stopped dead. The street was choked with people and carts and vehicles. What could they all be doing? Astra wondered uneasily. Surely everyone was not hoping to get to their train? It would have to be a very long one. Their father said they were certain to get on themselves since they had tickets. It was seven minutes to two on Hugo's watch.

Their two carts could progress no further; they were completely jammed in. No one in front would give way.

"You young ones go ahead," said Lukas Petersons. "Take the tickets. Get them to hold the train!"

With a quick look at Valdis—could this be the moment

that they were saying good-bye?—Astra raced off with Hugo, dodging in and out of the crowd. Tomas and Zigi followed hard on their heels. There were masses of people inside the station, too, standing around in groups, talking, gesticulating. More people were on the platform, gazing up the empty track. The train could not have come in yet. The children slowed and recovered their breath.

"Let's ask someone," said Astra.

"Isn't that Mr. Bergs, the stationmaster?" Hugo pointed to a small sandy-haired man in the middle of a knot of people. They were buzzing around him like angry wasps.

Hugo and Astra pushed their way through the throng, trying to reach him.

"Mr. Bergs!" Hugo stood on tiptoe and shouted over the tops of the people's heads. "The train to Riga?"

"It is gone."

"*Gone*?"

"It came in an hour ago and went straight out. It was packed full."

"An *hour* ago? But it couldn't have!"

"Well, it did! There is no such thing as a timetable now."

"But we have tickets." Hugo held them out.

"Tickets!" Mr. Bergs threw his hands up in the air.

"When is the next train?"

"There is no next train." The stationmaster was obviously at the end of his tether. "To anywhere. Perhaps there will be no more trains, ever!"

2

LUKAS went into the station to check for himself. But it was true—the train had gone.

"What are we going to do?" cried Astra, who had accompanied him.

Her father did not answer. He stood on the edge of the platform, staring at the point where the rail line curved and snaked out of sight. His head was cocked as if he were listening.

"Mr. Bergs seemed certain there would be no more trains," said Astra desperately, keeping her eyes on her father's face. He would know what to do, he always had. To some he seemed like an absentminded scholar, head buried in books, but she knew him to be ready to make decisions when he had to. "What are we going to do?" she asked again, but more gently.

"Turn around and go home—what else can we do?"

"Go home? But the Russians are coming!"

"We might as well be in our own house as sit on this platform when they arrive."

They pushed their way back through the crowds to where the families waited with the horses and carts.

Kristina said at once, "You can't go back, Lukas! You'll have to try to get a lift to Liepaja and wait for us there."

"Mrs. Petersons is right," said Paulis.

"And how are you all going to get to Liepaja?"

"Perhaps there'll be a train tomorrow."

Lukas shook his head. He said he would return home with them, then he would see.

The return journey was even slower. They were tired and apprehensive, and the horses seemed to be also, shying at every loud bang. The Germans and Russians were still warring on the horizon and every now and then a plane belonging to one or the other of them would swoop in low over their heads, sending them diving for cover. There was no time to wait and see what its markings were.

On this side of the road they had to pass the entrance to the military hospital where Lieutenant Schwarz worked. In the driveway stood a fleet of horses and carts of every shape and size. Crates and boxes were being hoisted on board and half a dozen German soldiers were running up and down, shouting orders.

"Wait here!" said Lukas.

They collapsed onto the grass at the side of the road. The Jansons' baby, Klara, was crying and would not stop no matter how much her mother rocked her, and Granny Jansons was muttering about mothers these days not being able to keep their children quiet. When hers were young she'd wrapped them up tight in a blanket so that they couldn't move either their arms or their legs and there had never been a squawk out of them.

Astra let her head fall back onto the grass. Valdis reclined on one elbow and looked down into her face. They regarded each other gravely. Astra felt as if her heart was about to burst open, like a seed pod exploding.

Lukas limped up the hospital drive. As he reached the top, Lieutenant Schwarz came out of the front door of the building. They greeted each other.

"So you're off today?" said Lukas.

The lieutenant nodded. "We expect the Russians to be here fairly soon. I'm leaving by truck in a few minutes with the last of the patients—the rest have already gone. But you, Herr Professor, I thought you would have gone by now?"

"We missed the train. It came in early. Could you help us at all, Herr Lieutenant? We're desperate, there's nowhere else for us to turn."

"I'd like to help you, you've been kind to me—"

Lukas dipped his head in acknowledgment.

"I'm not sure, though . . ." The lieutenant considered, his brows drawn together in a frown. "You might be able to go with our supply convoy to the coast. They're traveling by night, because of the air raids, so it will be hard going."

"Not as hard as staying."

"I'll have a word with the officer in charge. I'll tell him you're on the Russians' wanted list."

Lieutenant Schwarz disappeared inside, to return a few minutes later with the officer who said he'd be prepared to take them as long as they didn't overload the wagons. The amount of luggage they'd be allowed would be severely limited and the young children could ride, but the adults would have to walk unless they were elderly or disabled. Lukas flinched at the word "disabled" but had to accept that it applied to himself, for if he were to try to walk the more than two hundred miles he would end up as a liability. He thanked the officer, said his farewells to Lieutenant

Schwarz, wishing him a safe journey, and then went back to give the news to the others.

"We must take our things up to the hospital straight away."

Klavins and Valdis helped to carry their belongings up the drive. All the boxes would have to be left behind; they were too large and too heavy. Into a sack Kristina put five tin mugs and plates, a set of cutlery apiece, a kettle and frying pan, and to each member of her family she gave a thick, horsehair blanket. Olga Jansons did the same.

"Take the rest home with you, Klavins," said Lukas. "Make use of anything you wish."

"Thank you, Professor Petersons." The farmer stepped back. "We'd best say good-bye and be on our way." His voice was hoarse. He had known the Petersons and the Jansons all his life.

In turn, everyone came to shake hands with him and his son. Astra did not look into Valdis's face. She saw his square brown hand come out and clasp hers. His grip was strong. Then his hand dropped away and he turned to follow his father down the drive. Kristina put her arm around Astra's shoulders and held her close.

They sat on the steps of the hospital and waited. Darkness was creeping in around them, a light mist beginning to shroud the trees. The clatter of gunfire continued in the background, punctuated every now and then by an extra loud explosion. Their ears were so attuned to the noise that when it stopped they raised their heads to listen. The horses were becoming restive, tossing their heads and rattling their harnesses. Beside them, holding their heads, trying to quiet them, were Russian prisoners-of-war in bedraggled gray uniforms. They were to be the drivers. The Germans had no troops to spare.

Suddenly, there was a stir of activity around the side of

the building and a gaggle of cows, roped together, was led out and positioned at the back of the convoy. It seemed that they were coming, too.

"You can herd the cows, Tom!" said Hugo.

"We shan't make fast progress with those in tow," said Lukas drily. "And if we don't move soon we shall all be trapped." In the past hour the artillery fire had been heating up and there was a fiery tinge to the eastern sky.

"I think we should go home to our beds," said Granny Jansons. "My poor feet are perishing and I've forgotten my glasses."

"Your glasses were broken ages ago," said her daughter-in-law, but Granny went on lamenting, until it became like a dirge that almost sent them nodding off to sleep.

At last the officer in charge came riding out on a chestnut mare. His back was very straight. His spurs shone. Three other soldiers, hospital orderlies, were traveling on horseback also. The drivers climbed up onto the wagons and the officer told the civilians to spread themselves around as best they could.

Tomas was lifted onto a cart near the front. He felt cold and alone sitting up there beside this strange Russian soldier, who did not even look at him, but sat with the reins lying slackly between his hands, staring at the back of the horse's neck. Tomas clutched his rucksack to his stomach, glad to know that his one-eyed bear Bruno was safe inside it. He'd brought him along at the last moment, deciding that he didn't care if Zigi would think he was a baby. Twisting around, he saw that his mother was in the cart behind. She waved to him. His father, Zigi, Granny Jansons, Olga, and the baby were in other carts farther back. Astra and Hugo were walking, along with Mara and her father.

The officer cantered up to the head of the procession and raised his right arm. He was only an outline now against the gray-black sky. The horses began to inch forward and the cart wheels creaked under the heavy loads. They were on their way.

Tomas sniffed and wiped his nose with the back of his hand. He had told Bruno he was not going to cry, but in spite of that he could feel something warm and wet on his cheeks.

For the first part of the way Astra walked with Mara, linking arms. She talked and talked, about Valdis, how she loved him and he loved her and how when the war was over they'd come back and she would marry him.

"But you're only fourteen," said Mara. "You're just fourteen."

Just indeed! At least she was fourteen. Mara wouldn't be for another three months.

"We can wait—until I'm eighteen. Mother married Father when she was eighteen."

"Has he asked you?"

"No, but he will. I'm sure he will," Astra added, seeing the look of skepticism on her friend's face. What did Mara know about love! Astra withdrew her arm from Mara's but went on talking, having at times almost to shout, to compete with the noise of the artillery. It was constant. And from time to time a shell zoomed through the sky to explode not so very far away.

After a while Astra sighed and said no more. Her throat had dried up and she felt as if someone had punched her in the stomach. Her whole life was in turmoil.

Hugo walked alone, farther up the procession, keeping pace with the cart on which his younger brother rode. Tomas's head had dropped forward onto his chest. Beside him sat the Russian driver, hunched into his greatcoat, a bulkv black silhouette. Hugo spoke to him in Russian, asking his name. He had picked up a little Russian from his father, who spoke many languages.

The Russian turned his head, surprised, seemingly, to be spoken to, especially in his own tongue.

"Sergei," he replied.

"I am Hugo. How old are you, Sergei?"

"Eighteen."

"I am fourteen. Where are you from?"

"Leningrad."

"My father says it is a beautiful city."

Sergei nodded. "Very beautiful."

A flare lit up the road, making it seem as bright as day and revealing the long line of straggling wagons and plodding horses and the weary trudging people. How on earth would they ever get anywhere at all traveling at this rate? They would be on their knees before they got halfway to Liepaja. If a bomb or a shell didn't get them first. Which seemed more than likely. And if they did get to Liepaja, would they find a ship prepared to take them?

We have become refugees now, thought Hugo. The full impact of what had happened to them was just beginning to register—they had become homeless, without a roof over their heads, without possessions or means of support. They were people on a road going wherever the wind of fate might blow them. And in what strange company were they making their journey—with German medical orderlies and Russian prisoners-of-war!

Another flare flashed, and he glanced around. Astra was sprinting up the side of the convoy, her hair flying out behind her. She caught up with him and slipped her hand into his.

They were relieved to see the first smudges of pale pink light in the sky—the sign of a new day dawning. The young children were fast asleep, bent over their bundles, looking like rag dolls. The walkers had begun to stumble. At intervals throughout the night several convoys of German armed trucks traveling with masked headlights and one of tanks had come rolling through and they'd had to move quickly onto the side of the road. They'd heard the rumble of wheels and seen the flash of steel as the vehicles had swept past. They'd seemed like machines from another planet: such speed amazed them—they who were traveling at a snail's pace. Their world had slowed down and the night hours had seemed interminable. Time and distance had become concepts difficult to grasp.

As dawn spread across the eastern sky and color was beginning to seep back into the land around them, the German officer on the chestnut mare led the way into a big old birch wood. They were to encamp here during the day and then move on again once darkness fell.

The paths were soft underfoot. There was a smell of damp earth and leafmold. In a clearing, Lukas and Paulis spread tarpaulins for their families, and then the travelers rolled in a horsehair blanket, curled up close together, lying front to back, like spoons, to contain their body heat.

This was to be the pattern of their days and nights.

Waking several hours later, stiff and chilled, Astra looked up to see a parasol of green and yellow leaves spread overhead against the blue sky. Birch trees! Some things were unchanged. The sun was shining on the topmost leaves, making them appear to shimmer and dance. She had always loved birch trees, ever since she was a little girl, because of the way they shimmered. And she loved their shiny, silver-white, elegant trunks. She forgot the discomfort in her body. How could the world still look so beautiful when such terrible things were going on? Even now, while the sun was turning the leaves to gold, she could hear the bombardment of the guns. The sound of killing.

Moving gingerly, trying not to disturb Tomas and Hugo who lay on either side of her, she eased herself out of her blanket roll and stood up, stretching herself to ease the stiffness from her limbs. Tomas rolled over onto her abandoned blanket, one arm flung up above his head. Hugo slept on, his face buried in its covering, only a tuft of fair hair showing. She saw that he had placed his glasses carefully on the ground, a foot from his head, their stems crossed. He had to be very careful with his glasses; without them, he was semi-blind. Then she saw that there was another space, where her father had lain.

She found him sitting on a tree stump a few yards away, smoking his pipe. The smell of the tobacco seemed reassuring, familiar, although at home they had always complained and said, "That filthy pipe!" As the war had gone on and it had become more and more difficult to get tobacco, the smells had become filthier. She sat down beside him.

The convoy was scattered throughout the wood and most people still seemed to be sleeping or at least reluctant to emerge from their cocoons. The prisoners-of-war were all together in one clearing, lying higgeldy-piggeldy on the ground, with one of the German soldiers on guard. He sat with his back against a tree, his eyes closed, his rifle across his knees.

The animals were loose, wandering about, cropping grass. The cows were lowing.

"They need to be milked," said Lukas.

They saw the officer coming through the trees. His uniform looked less smart than it had when he had ridden out at their head the night before and his boots were muddied to the ankles. He was looking for people to milk the cows.

"We can help," said Lukas.

The Petersons and Jansons all knew how to milk. The five young ones set to, enlivened to have something to do, although as Astra leaned her head against the cow's warm flank and watched the bluish-white milk squirting down into the bucket she could think only of Valdis and her sadness deepened again.

The young boys were having a competition.

"My cow's given more milk than yours," shouted Zigi.

"No, mine has! Look!" cried Tomas and spilled it, all over his trouser legs. He was to smell of sour milk for the next two days.

On the fifth morning, they came upon an abandoned farmhouse. A cow was tethered up in the backyard and hens were flurrying around, pecking at the earth.

"Today we shall have a roof over our heads," said the officer. "And we shall have eggs and a hen or two for the pot."

Each family was given a room to itself. The Petersons' was an upstairs bedroom that had once been slept in by a child. Dolls and teddy bears were seated with their legs splayed out on the narrow bed. Their china and button eyes looked bright and alert as if they were watching for their owner's return.

"You take the bed, Kristina," said Lukas firmly. "The rest of us will be comfortable on the floor. There are even rugs, for goodness sake!"

Tomas was asleep, Bruno tucked in under his chin, before the rest had time to settle down. Tomas's cheeks looked flushed, his mother observed as she bent over him, but her husband said she should not fuss and get some sleep. "It's the fresh air, it's giving us all rosy cheeks." He was growing a beard himself; it was not possible to shave, anyway.

Kristina remained anxious about Tomas, getting up and

down to check him during the night, as did Hugo. On the previous day's journey, Sergei, the Russian driver, had said to him, "I think young Tom is sick. He reminds me of my young brother Alexei when he had a fever." Tomas tossed and turned and by morning was clearly feverish and running a high temperature. And so, it turned out, was Zigi, in the next room. Their mothers talked on the landing and came to the conclusion that it might be scarlet fever.

Lukas conferred with his older children. "I'm wondering whether to speak to the captain and ask if we might stay for a day or two."

"But he might just decide to leave us behind," said Astra. "I don't suppose he'll want to hold the convoy up."

Lukas sighed. "The trouble is that Tom and Zigi are not fit to travel the way they are at present."

As he spoke, they heard a rush of noise, announcing the arrival of a bomber overhead, and in the next instant, before they had time to move, there was a great bang and the house shook. The blast pitched them sideways. A chunk of plaster fell from the ceiling and dust rained down.

"What's happened?" cried Tomas, delirious, thrashing about on the bed. "Have they come for us?"

"No, it's all right, Tom," said Astra softly and crawled over to him. She stroked his forehead, which felt as if it were on fire. What if Tom were to die? *Please God,* she whispered inside her head, *please God, don't let Tom die.* She knew it could happen. Since this dreadful war had started she had come to realize that anything was possible.

Her father and Hugo had scrambled to their feet and were standing in silence at the window. She went to join them.

"Keep back, Astra!" Her father put out his arm to bar her way.

"What is it? Let me see!" She pushed between them and looked down. The bomb had landed in the farmyard where the prisoners-of-war had been camped out. A number were dead—the bits of bodies lying around made it difficult to assess the number—and all the rest were injured.

They stayed three days and two nights in the farmhouse. During that time the dead were buried in the field behind the house and the injured brought in and laid out in rows on the sitting room floor. The Petersons and Jansons helped the German orderlies bathe and dress their wounds. Hugo proved to be the most adept; he had deft yet soothing hands, and he did not flinch at the sight of blood and exposed bone. He spoke gently to the wounded in their own language and they subsided, entrusting themselves to him. Hugo had healing hands, said their father, who was clumsy himself with bandages, winding them too tightly or too loosely so that they did not stay in place. Hugo thought he might like to be a doctor when he grew up, unlike Astra, who could hardly bear to look at some of the wounds and had to run outside to be sick.

Tomas's driver, Sergei, had been injured. His left arm had been blown off and his right leg shot to pieces.

"Tom—how is he?" Sergei asked when he came out of his delirium. He was very weak and Hugo thought he could not last more than a day or two. He could feel the life force ebbing out of Sergei's body when he held him.

"Oh, Tom's much better. He's sitting up in bed coloring a picture."

It was a picture of the black horse that drew Sergei's cart. Tomas had drawn a red bow tied to one ear. The drawing had verve and conveyed a sense of movement and character. In this respect, Tomas took after their mother, who had studied art as a girl and always kept a sketchbook in her pocket. She worked away in it during the long spells of inactivity. It helped her to stay sane, she said, and it would be a record of their journey.

Hugo brought the picture down to Sergei later.

For Sergei, Tomas had written in large letters across the top.

"Thank you." A smile crossed Sergei's lips. Hugo gave him some water from a cup, helping him to sit up and drink.

"I would like to go home," said Sergei in an unexpectedly strong voice.

"I know," said Hugo. "We all would."

And it was at that moment that Sergei died, in Hugo's arms.

After their sojourn at the farmhouse, they moved on in a somber mood, leaving the dead with roughly hewn wooden crosses to mark their graves and the wounded Russian prisoners-of-war in the care of one another.

"We can't take them with us," said the German officer. "It's out of the question."

"I expect the Russians will be here soon, anyway," said Lukas to the children, who were concerned. "They can't be far away."

They had no way of knowing exactly where the Soviets were—it was almost impossible to estimate their position from the sound of the action, as the front was not a fixed line moving in steadily like a tidal wave; it ebbed and eddied all the time. And the officer was receiving no intelligence from anywhere; he had lost touch with his command post and only knew that he must slog along in the hopes of reaching Liepaja with his convoy, which was daily looking more ragged. Five carts had had to be abandoned due to lack of drivers; the rest were entrusted to Lukas and Paulis and their older children. Hugo took up

Sergei's reins, with Tomas swaddled in rugs on the seat beside him. Both of the boys had been greatly saddened by Sergei's death.

"I hardly knew him," Hugo said to Astra, after they had buried the Russian boy. "But I'll never forget him. He died in *my* arms."

3

FIVE WEEKS after leaving home—an eternity, so it seemed to them—they arrived in the port of Liepaja to embark on the next stage of their journey, down the coast of Lithuania through the Baltic Sea to the Gulf of Danzig. For two weeks they had stayed a few miles inland at a relief camp run by Latvians. They'd had to sleep on the floor, but at least they'd had the chance to rest their feet and wash themselves and their clothes.

Riga had fallen to the Soviets: they had heard that while they were in the camp. And the country north of it, also. Russian soldiers might now be trampling through their house, sleeping in their beds. They had left just in time.

The docks of Liepaja were teeming with refugees and German soldiers. Some of the soldiers were wounded and lay slumped against one another moaning, their wounds wrapped in newspaper. The Germans had run out of bandages. Ships were being loaded up, with military supplies and hardware, horses, carts, trailers, soldiers. If there was room, once the military requirements had been met, the refugees would be taken, too. They waited anxiously throughout the night. The harbor rang with the sound of horses' hooves and the drumming of men's booted feet, the shout of orders and the crying of young children and of the sick and elderly.

"I'm amazed that they're even considering taking us," said Hugo to his father. "Why should they bother?"

"I suppose because we're fleeing from the Russians—a common enemy! Though I doubt that we can be a high priority!"

The refugees huddled on the quayside trying to keep warm under pieces of sacking, cardboard, paper, anything they could lay hands on. The night was long and cold, and the wind coming off the sea, bitter. Tomas and Zigi stamped up and down with seemingly limitless energy.

"I'm getting electric shocks," cried Tomas, doing a little tap dance.

"It must be the nails in your boots," said Hugo.

Tomas and Zigi went on striking the soles of their boots across the ground and shrieking when the shocks made their feet tingle. Then they chased each other up and down, playing tag, dodging in and out of the groups of people, being cursed by some. Don't go too far away, Lukas cautioned them. *Never* go too far away.

"Tom and Zigi can still forget what is going on," said Astra wistfully. "At least for short spells."

She had been poking with a stick in a puddle of mud, scratching out letters. Even in the poor light Hugo could see that she had written the name Valdis.

They threw themselves to the ground as they heard a whine in the sky. A few seconds later two red-starred planes were overhead wheeling and diving, tipping their wings toward the sea and the ships. Bombs rained into the water. One struck a small tug. And then three Messerschmits appeared and the Russians veered about and went scudding off eastward, chased by the Germans.

The refugees lifted their heads again. Air raids had become so commonplace that they reacted automatically, and when one was ended they picked themselves up and resumed whatever they had been doing.

In the morning they were told they could board the ships. People flocked to the gangways, carrying bundles and babies in their arms, shouldering small children; they pressed forward, desperate not to be left behind.

"Keep close together," Lukas Petersons reminded his family yet again. "Come on, Tom, hang on to my belt."

Inch by inch, they progressed up the swaying gangway to the already crowded decks. Tomas said he was sure the ship was going to sink, he could feel it. "I can, too!" cried Zigi. They were told to hush. Hugo took a deep breath and fixed his eyes on the back of Astra's head. Crowds made him feel claustrophobic. He had had a fear of them as a small child that he had never managed to get rid of—it had started when he had tripped and fallen in a crowded Riga department store one Christmas. He'd lain on the ground, terrified, while enormous feet had gone trampling over him until his father's strong hands had reached down and rescued him. He could only have lain for a minute but it had been long enough for the incident to leave its mark. It would not be possible to fall down in the middle of this crowd, however. At times they ceased to move but stood, locked solid, a mass of heaving bodies.

Lukas pushed on, using his shoulders to open up a passage, and led them below where they found enough space in a hold to make a small encampment. They seated themselves in a ring, with their possessions in the center. It was like a magic ring, Tomas said, making his mother smile.

"That's right," she said. "And if we stay inside it we shall be safe."

Soon the hold filled up and the air became hot and close. They felt the boat shifting and lurching beneath them.

"I think we might have set sail," said Lukas.

Granny Jansons was singing a lament about the sea now. The sea was meant for fish and not for men and women. Certainly not for women. Men perhaps, so that they could go out and catch the fish. But the women had always stayed at home. She should have stayed at home. She hated the sea. One or two other old people were moaning, babies were crying, someone was retching and being sick on the other side. The stench was appalling and seemed to fill the entire hold and started other people retching, too. Astra began to wish that they had stayed on deck and braved the cold Baltic wind. Shut your eyes, ears, and mouths, like the three wise monkeys, said their mother, and try to go to sleep. It was the best advice.

They had learned to sleep easily, anywhere. One by one, the heads drooped, even Granny Jansons'. Lukas, though, could not sleep; nor Hugo.

"Shall we see if we can get up on deck for a breath of air?" suggested Lukas.

They had to climb over sleeping bodies, crawl over bundles and boxes, but at length they reached the deck. Hugo thought he had never smelled anything as fine as the fresh salt air. He inhaled a lungful and his head seemed to clear. The wind whipped their hair back and cooled their heated faces.

"It's good, isn't it?" said his father.

Hugo nodded.

The port of Liepaja could no longer be seen—Latvia was behind them. They had not been on deck to take a last look at their country. Perhaps it was just as well, said Lukas. On their left lay the coast of Lithuania. They could expect Russian bombers to come from that direction.

They were traveling in a convoy. Their ship was third in a line of five. The sea was swelling slightly and the deck rolling a little, but not drastically. Hugo and Lukas held on to the rail and watched the bow as it cut its way through the steel-gray sea, sending out flurries of white around it. The sea was soothing, almost hypnotic, thought Hugo, as he stared straight down into it.

"Look, Hugo!" His father was nudging him and pointing.

Hugo wiped the spray from his glasses and gazed farther out to sea.

"See that black speck?"

Hugo frowned, then he saw it. "Yes. What can it be?"

"I think it might be a submarine."

The captain seemed to think so, also, for an alarm bell was pealing out and sailors, their path blocked by people, were struggling to get to their stations. Hugo and his father kept watching the black speck until they thought it had disappeared altogether. Their eyes were beginning to blur. But when they blinked they saw that the black mark was still there, standing up like a spike. And from it, coming straight toward them, was a white streak. They gazed, mesmerized, unable to do anything but stand and stare. Hugo had never seen a torpedo before but he knew that that was what it must be.

Everything else happened very fast. The captain shouted from the bridge overhead and the ship appeared to change course. The deck tilted sideways, sending shrieking passengers sliding into a heap. The torpedo came boring steadily on, plowing through the choppy sea—to miss them! It passed no more than six feet away, on the starboard side, which was where Hugo and his father stood. They stared after the disappearing missile.

"That was a near one!" the captain shouted to an officer below.

So intent were they on watching the progress of the torpedo that they had not registered the arrival of a plane overhead. It was a Russian fighter and it was coming in low over their heads. The ship's guns roared into action and the vessel lurched again. The noise was deafening.

"Hold on!" shouted Lukas.

They saw the bomb leaving the plane, an elongated steel-gray object, and in the next instant the ship was sent rocking and bucking, like a cork in a whirlpool. Hugo and Lukas held on tightly to the rail as they were pitched first one way and then the other. People were screaming. Astra, Mother, Tom, thought Hugo—they are trapped below. He could see them spread out in front of him, their arms held wide, their eyes turned up to his, beseeching him to save them. It is said that, sometimes, at the moment of death or near-death one sees one's whole life flash in front of one. Perhaps one also sees one's family. The moment seemed to go on and on, as if time was winding down like a film at the cinema when the projector is about to give up. Any second now there might be a scramble of black lines on the screen, a flash of light, and then darkness.

But instead, miraculously, the ship seemed to right itself. It still went on bobbing like a cork, but like one in a bathtub rather than in a whirlpool. Hugo and Lukas saw that their arms and legs were shaking uncontrollably. They rested their backs against the deck rail. They were unable to speak.

The bomb must have just missed them. Lucky twice in a row! To be lucky three times might be more than they could hope for. The ship's guns had got the plane: it had vanished from the sky and what looked like its wreckage floated half a mile or so away.

Then they heard a sharp crack which sounded like an

explosion from up ahead. They turned to look. Black smoke was pouring from the ship leading the convoy and flames were licking along its deck. The submarine had scored a hit.

Surviving attacks from above and below, they picked their way for a day and a night through the perilous seas of the Baltic and, on the first of November, steamed into the port of Gdynia in German-occupied Poland. From there they hoped to get a train into Germany.

It was a gray, overcast day. A typical November day, said Kristina, but she tried to say it brightly as if she did not mind that the sun was not shining. They were glad to disembark and leave the stinking hold behind. They were glad, also, to be away from the constant threat of submarines and air raids; they'd felt so exposed out there in the middle of the sea with nowhere to turn. They'd been badly shaken when the leading ship of their convoy had been torpedoed. No survivors had been found. When they'd steamed past the wreckage they'd seen bodies bobbing up and down in the waves.

"I'm rolling when I walk," said Tomas. "Look!" And he capered about, walking in an exaggerated way and falling about, making Zigi laugh.

"Don't get separated from us," said Lukas sharply. "Stay in close now, Tom! How many times do I have to tell you?"

Tomas dropped into line behind his father and the others followed on, Kristina after Tomas, then came Astra, with Hugo bringing up the rear. The Jansons made up a similar formation. The crowds were dense again. They moved, a huge press of people, to the railway sidings where trains stood. They drew in to the side and paused to take stock.

"Will there be a train going directly to Leipzig?" Astra asked her father.

"I doubt it. We'll have to try to get to Berlin and change

there." Lukas hailed a passing railway official and spoke to him in German. "Excuse me, do any of these trains go to Berlin?"

"Berlin?" The man looked at him as if he had asked for the moon. "We don't know where any of them are going to. They're refugee trains."

"But aren't they going *somewhere*?"

"No known destinations. To camps in other parts of Poland, or Germany." The man shrugged. "Depends where they can get the refugees taken in. Best get on one while you can." He hurried away.

"I suppose we'd better do what he says," said Lukas. "We don't seem to have much choice." He passed a hand over his eyes. "We no longer seem to be in charge of our own lives—we have to face up to that."

"It might be possible to connect with a train for Berlin or Leipzig later," said Hugo.

"Let's go!" said Kristina. They were being pushed farther and farther to the side by the ongoing rush of people. "Otherwise we might be left behind."

They moved back into the mainstream. Astra kept her eyes on her mother's head. Don't lose sight of the one in front of you, their father had stressed, not even for a second. A second was long enough in which to lose someone in the middle of a milling crowd. The throng buffeted and tugged at her and a man pushed roughly between her and her mother and for more than a second Astra did lose sight of Kristina's fair head with its French knot lying on the nape of her neck. And in that space of time Astra felt panic rise up in her like a tide of sickness welling from the pit of her stomach, and she shoved the person in front of her aside and pressed forward with all her strength, not caring if she banged into someone or trod on his toes. She almost fainted with relief when she saw the familiar head bobbing no more than two feet away. Her heart was pounding. Silly thing! she told herself. You can't lose people that easily.

Lukas had found a carriage near the front of one of the trains and was holding open the door. They climbed up, throwing their baggage up onto the rack.

"Is there room for all of us?" asked Paulis.

"Of course! Quickly, everyone in! I can see a conductor with a whistle up ahead. I don't suppose they'll hang about once the train is full."

Granny Jansons was helped up the high step and pulled in. "Where are we going now?" she demanded.

No one answered.

"Father," said Astra, frowning. "Father, where is Hugo?"

Lukas took a quick look around the compartment and then lowered himself onto the ground again. Astra jumped down beside him. There were still dozens of people working their way up the train hoping to find free spaces. A conductor was coming along, too, slamming carriage doors.

"I expect he'll be along in a moment," said Lukas, scanning the faces of the refugees. "He'll find us. It's not as if he's four years old."

The conductor was waving to them, insistently, indicating that they should get inside. At once! A whistle was shrilling. It pierced their ears through the babble of voices. What were they to do?

"We can't go without Hugo, Father," cried Astra. "*We can't!*"

The whistle shrieked again. The engine was throbbing into life, gushing out steam.

"He's sure to have got on at the back of the train," said Lukas, his eyes straining as they searched the crowd. "He couldn't have been that far behind us."

The whistle shrilled a third time.

Kristina and Tomas were at the open door of the compartment, watching with anxious eyes.

"Shall we jump out, Lukas?" called Kristina.

"No, stay there! You can't all get off now." The train was beginning to move. "Get on, Astra, we *have* to get on!"

Lukas Petersons pushed his daughter hard in the middle of the back, propelling her forward, and she was forced to leap on board. She grazed her knee as she landed. She scrambled up and turned to help her father. His right leg was weak and he could not get it high enough. It was trailing behind him and all the time the train was gathering speed and the end of the siding was coming up and the open track stretched in front of them. His left foot was on the step, but slipping. Astra and Paulis seized him by the shoulders and, mustering all their strength, dragged him into the compartment. They collapsed in a heap on the floor between the rows of legs.

Every carriage was close-packed; the corridors, also. She would never be able to make her way down the train, Lukas told Astra, who had opened the door of their compartment. She looked directly into the face of a man. Bristles of hair stuck out over his chin, making it look like a ragged porcupine. His mouth was slightly open and she could smell his breath, hot and stale. He was watching her through narrowed eyes, as if he might be getting ready to jump into her place should she vacate it.

"Wait till we get to our destination, dear," said her mother, her voice not quite steady. "I'm sure we'll find Hugo then."

"Is Hugo lost?" asked Tomas.

"Of course not! He's had to get on farther back, that's all.

And if he didn't then he'd make his way to Professor Zimmermann's in Leipzig."

"I can't wait," declared Astra, and saying "Excuse me" to the man who was staring at her, she attempted to push past him. For an instant their bodies were wedged together, stuck, as if by suction, then she wriggled and heaved and was past him, to confront another woman like a wall before her. The porcupine man was trying to get into their compartment and Paulis was barring his way telling him that Astra would be coming back shortly.

"I can't breathe out here." The man was angry.

Few were in good temper or particularly helpful; if they'd fought for their patch they felt they had a right to stand their ground. It had to be every man and woman for himself and herself. Who could afford to be philanthropic? Astra kept on repeating "Excuse me" and "I'm looking for my brother—my *twin* brother" and trying to push her way down the train. She asked if anyone had seen a boy of fourteen with fair hair and glasses—"Round glasses, with steel frames. He blinks quite a bit"—and they looked at her as if she were crazy. Who would have time to notice if someone blinked? And there must be fifty boys with glasses on the train. One woman said everyone was looking for someone. A man said he was looking for his wife. He spoke mournfully and with resignation, as if he did not expect ever to find her again. He looked dead at the back of the eyes. But some people were kind and sucked in their breath to make themselves smaller so that Astra could squeeze past and said, "Your brother, dear? It would be an awful thing to lose a brother. Especially a twin brother."

Hugo was not in the first three carriages. Needing air and a rest from pushing and shoving and having her feet trampled on and trying not to trample on other people's feet, she stopped by an open window and leaned out. She watched brown-and-white cows going past and a tree standing alone in the middle of a field with a spillage of yellow leaves strewn around its base and now a gray horse with a white marking on its forehead, cropping grass. It raised its head, shaking its mane, and gazed solemnly at the train while continuing to chew. Astra saw each thing clearly: the train was creeping along at little more than walking pace. She was tempted to jump out and run beside it, but if she were to do this, it would be certain to get up a head of steam and go streaking off, leaving her behind. An image of herself standing by the empty track flashed in front of her eyes. She squared her shoulders and pressed on through the sea of bodies.

So many heads, so many people; some boys of Hugo's age with fair hair, but none with steel spectacles. No one looking a little bit like an owl, whose gray eyes would light up behind their glass screens when they met hers. No one who would know what she was thinking without having to ask.

And then she saw him, sitting at the end of the corridor, with his knees up, his head resting on them, cradled by his arms. He seemed to be sleeping.

"Hugo!" she cried.

He did not stir.

She struggled on until she was within touching distance. Reaching out her hand, she tapped him on the shoulder.

"Hey, you!"

His head jerked up and he looked around. It was not Hugo.

HUGO had been keeping Astra firmly in his line of vision, had woven in and out of the crowd behind her, when an arm had come up, caught the edge of his spectacles, and sent them flying. They soared in a wide arc over his head and dropped from sight.

"Please," he said, pushing and elbowing, trying to prise open a hole in the middle of the multitude so that he could get down and retrieve the two round pieces of glass that meant for him the difference between seeing and not seeing. "Please . . ." His hands groped wildly, encountering only the solid backs of moving people.

No one heard, no one had time to listen. They surged on, anxious to reach the trains, determined not to be left behind. Hugo, swept up in their midst, was carried along, and so, too, were his glasses, for as he peered down through the swarm of legs he glimpsed a flash of light that he knew instinctively must be them. They were being propelled forward by the hurrying, scurrying, relentless feet. And then he saw a heavy boot lift up and come down flat to obliterate the blink of light and in the same instant he heard the nauseating scrunch of breaking glass, even above the noisy trample of feet. It was a sound that would have reached his ears through the most deafening of thunderstorms. His eyes were being put out! He made a desperate lunge downward causing the throng to eddy and part for a moment, then it closed ranks again and moved on, leaving him where he had fallen. On his way down, he felt the feet—on his back, shoulders, head. The nightmare had returned.

Surfacing into consciousness, he was aware of a whistle blowing in the distance and the *chug-chug-chug* of an engine growing gradually fainter. The sounds seemed to be coming from far, far away, and were overlaid by the gabble of voices and the rapid tattoo of the desperate feet. He struggled to get up, fell back.

"It's all right, lad, hold on!" said a voice, and a strong pair of hands lifted him under the armpits and helped him to sit up.

"The train—" Hugo spoke with difficulty. Somewhere in the depths of his muddled head he knew that he should be on the train, that Astra was on it, and his mother and father and Tomas. His family. "I must go—" He collapsed again.

"There are other trains," said the man, in Latvian.

"Maris, we *must* get on a train," said a woman. "We can't afford to delay." A whistle went. "Look, that's another one going!"

Blinking, Hugo saw the fuzzy outline of a woman standing in front of him, holding a small child by either hand. She was bending toward him, though he could not make out her face.

"That's a nasty-looking head wound," she said.

"I'll help him onto the train," said the man and Hugo felt himself being heaved up until his feet scraped the ground. "Can you walk, lad? Try to. Here, lean on me. You go on, Silvia, and see if you can find some seats."

The man, whose name was Maris, half dragged, half carried Hugo along the siding to the train. Silvia was calling, "Here, Maris, here!" Other hands reached down and pulled Hugo up into a compartment. He was given a seat in the corner, and something soft was put behind his head. He saw a sea of blurred faces whirling around and around. He had to close his eyes to shut them out. Take a drink, said another woman's voice and liquid trickled into his mouth and down his chin. Yet another woman, with gentle hands, dabbed at his forehead, saying the cut was deep, it should be stitched, he was losing a lot of blood. He felt as if it were all happening to someone else.

The train traveled westward, crossing the Polish border into Germany. Sometimes it picked up speed; sometimes it dropped back again, and every now and then they stopped and sat for an hour or so, or more, sometimes for no apparent reason, but often so that trains bearing the military could go charging through. Then they were shunted into sidings to wait until the train with priority had flashed past, compartments jammed with soldiers, wagons bristling with armaments.

When the train stopped the passengers got out, a few at a time, always leaving several in their compartment to guard their places. And they kept watchful eyes on the engine driver who also climbed down from his cab to take a break. They walked up and down beside the track to stretch their legs and took advantage of nearby woods—the train toilets were in a foul state when passengers did manage to battle their way along the corridor to them. And every few hours they drew into a station where relief agencies were waiting to dispense food: bread, a bit of hard cheese, and sometimes milk for the younger children.

Hugo was unable to eat anything but took a few sips of

water when a cup was put to his mouth. He slept or slipped into unconsciousness much of the time. Sometimes, wakening, he found that he could follow snatches of the conversations going on around him. None of the voices belonged to anyone in his family. He listened carefully to see if they did.

There was a great deal of talk about where they might be going. Someone had heard Bavaria, another Hamburg.

"I don't think anyone knows. Not even the engine drivers or the conductors."

"That's true! And the station officials don't seem to have any idea, either. They just send us on, wanting to get rid of us!"

"They must have their hands full with the Russians pressing them so hard."

"I wish the war would end soon!" said a woman's voice. "I would like to go to America and live with my brother. He has a good job and a nice house in Minnesota."

America! They fell silent at the thought. They might as well think of going to the moon. Before the war had started Hugo had seen some American films in which the people had lived in beautiful houses and had worn beautiful clothes, and the sun had shone all day. He seemed to remember a melody from one of the films, yet could not quite grasp it. He thought he could hear someone humming the tune. He tried to join in. But he had never been able to sing in tune. Now Astra had a fine voice, had always been picked to sing the solos in the school choir.

"Astra," he said, sitting up and opening his eyes to stare around the compartment. He could not see her. Where could she be?

"It's all right." Maris wiped his forehead with a damp cloth. "Lie back and try not to fret."

Hugo closed his eyes again. The voices carried on.

"They will let you go to friends or relatives if you have

any," a woman said. "In Germany, I mean. Not America!" She laughed.

"Maris and I are hoping to go to my cousin in Neustrelitz," said Silvia.

"That's if the train goes through there, Silvia," cautioned Maris.

"But we're heading that way, aren't we?"

Leipzig! thought Hugo. The name had come to him out of the fog in his head. But what was it that he should remember about Leipzig? Whatever it was it was lost in the swirls of mist that were beginning to engulf his brain again.

At one station a nurse came on board and cleaned up his wound as best she could. But there was not much she could do except try to pull it together with adhesive tape and bind it tightly.

"There's a hospital nearby, but it's full with the military." She gave him a small box of tablets to help the pain, and a spare bandage. "Put them in your bag. Do you have a bag?"

Hugo could not remember.

"It must have got left behind at Gdynia," said Maris. "In the crush."

"What a shame!" said Silvia. "All his possessions!"

The nurse tucked the box and the bandage into Hugo's coat pocket.

The next station they came into after that was Neustrelitz. Silvia jumped up excitedly.

"It may not stop," said Maris. The train began to brake.

"Children, put on your coats, pick up your bags, don't forget anything!" cried Silvia.

The rest watched enviously. Hugo opened his eyes to see what all the excitement was about.

The train shuddered to a stop.

"Let's go, Maris! We mustn't miss our chance."

Maris squatted down in front of Hugo and looked into his

face. "We have to go, lad. I'm sorry we can't take you with us but my wife's cousin has only a small house and—" He shrugged.

I am a stranger, thought Hugo, his mind lucid at that moment; I am not his kin.

Maris's hand grasped his. "Look after yourself. I expect the others will help you."

I have lost my kin, thought Hugo, his fingers groping for Maris's.

"Maris!"

"I'm coming."

Hugo saw Maris leap down onto the platform and disappear, his friend of a few hours, but the only friend that he had in this terrifying new world.

After three days and nights on the train, punctuated by long, frequent stops and several air raids, they came to yet another halt and were told to disembark. There was no sign of any habitation. They couldn't be too far from Hamburg, one of the men reckoned, perhaps about nine miles. He'd been trying to follow their zigzag progress on his map. Hugo was helped down from the compartment. He sank on to the grassy bank beside the track. The air was cold and damp. Children were crying.

The conductor told them they were going to a refugee camp nearby. They must walk, along the side of the track to begin with, and then on paths across fields. "It's about a half mile or so, maybe a little more." He pointed and their eyes swiveled toward the horizon where the camp could be seen crouching: a sprawling collection of wooden huts that had once been used as a summer camp for schoolchildren.

It was raining slightly and beginning to darken as they set out. Two men linked arms with Hugo and assisted him along the track. He struggled to keep up, not to hold them back. He knew it was imperative not to hold people back; everyone wanted to hurry, everyone was fearful of being left behind. The families of the two men kept glancing back and then they'd look around to see that the distance between them and the people out in front had widened. Already some were halfway across the fields. They could be seen against the skyline, heads lowered into the wind, backs bent under their bundles, pressing onward.

"Let me rest a bit," Hugo gasped. The effort to come those few yards had drained him, and the camp still looked a long way away. "I'll be all right if I can just rest." He slumped back down onto the bank. In his mind was forming the vague idea that, if he were to sit here for a while, sooner or later, the train bearing his family might come through.

"We can't leave you here," one of the men objected. "Listen, I tell you what—you stay and rest and get your strength up and we'll come back for you after we've settled our families. Okay?"

Hugo nodded, and the men went on.

The rain thickened into a downpour. Hugo had no energy to seek shelter. There was little, anyway, by the side of the railway track, and the trees in the field behind were almost bare, except for a few tattered leaves that were hanging as if by threads. He lay sprawled against the bank, the cold November rain beating down on him, soaking his clothes, his hair, his bandage. The sharp drops flailed his eyeballs under their closed lids. He felt as if he were lying under a waterfall. There was a waterfall in the river back home, a gentle, playful one that gurgled and sparkled as it splashed from stone to stone. On hot days they'd cup their hands beneath it and bring up palmfuls of cool water to their mouths and drink deep, slaking their thirst. He ran his tongue around his lips and sucked in the rain. The moisture felt good to his parched mouth. How odd that his mouth should be so hot when every other part of him was so cold.

He half opened his eyes and made an attempt to raise his head. Something peculiar was happening to the ground underneath him. It seemed to be trembling—to be moving! Was it an earthquake? But earthquakes happened in hot places, didn't they? He thought that they did. He was confused. He remembered his primary school teacher Mr. Roze telling them about an earthquake somewhere in America. California? He couldn't remember, though he could see Mr. Roze, with a long pointer in his hand, standing in front of the big map of the world that had hung on the back of the schoolroom wall. There was a terrible rumble coming from somewhere and it was getting louder and louder and soon it was going to burst his eardrums. He tried to bring his hands up to cover his ears, but his arms would not obey the command. They fell limply back against the bank.

The blast of the passing engine sent his body into a convulsion. When he lay still again he saw, through the slanting rain, what he thought might be smoke, and a shower of orange sparks. It was a train! Of course it was a train! He had seen trains before. He had traveled in them. He managed to raise his head an inch or two, blinking as each carriage streaked past. Zoom, zoom, zoom! They seemed to whisk by in a flash.

Astra . . . He thought he saw her, sitting at a window, her head resting sideways on her hand, her straight, fair hair hanging like a shaft of light. He thought he saw her eyes, gray, like cool pebbles at the bottom of the stream. He thought he heard her voice saying his name. He tried to answer, to say her name, but his head fell back. He could see nothing but a gray blur. And he could no longer hear the train. The only sound in his ears was the steady drumming of the rain, and after a while, that, too, faded.

5

WHENEVER they approached a station, Astra felt hope fluttering in her anew. Hugo might be there. He might have come in on another train. It wasn't impossible, was it?

"You can't expect that, dear," said her mother quietly. "If he got on another train it must be behind ours."

"But it might have passed while we were in a siding."

"That's doubtful," said her father.

"If he's behind us why don't we get off and wait for the next train?"

"We wouldn't be allowed to. No, we've just got to hope that either he will catch up with us somewhere or we shall meet up in Berlin or Leipzig."

Astra questioned the relief workers at the stations. They were working long hours and were weary, had seen many refugees of many nationalities—Estonians, Latvians, Lithuanians, German nationals from Poland and Czechoslovakia fleeing from the Russians—and they could not remember boys with or without steel spectacles.

"If you do come across a boy called Hugo Petersons—a Latvian boy—would you tell him that we were here?"

Somewhere in the middle of Germany their train halted for several hours. The area had been badly bombed; little had been left standing. Factories, houses, schools, churches—all had been flattened. People were wandering about amid the rubble looking dazed. Some sat, faces gray with dust, not moving. Others tried to get on their train.

"We are Latvian refugees," Lukas told them. "There is no point in coming with us."

There was no room, either.

Lukas walked along the track to find the Latvian minister who had been put nominally in charge of the train.

"They're going to reroute us, apparently," Pastor Vizulis said, "since not much is left standing here. The Allied bombers are devastating the German cities. So they're going to send us back into Poland."

"Poland? But that will take us toward the Russian lines again!"

No one wants us, thought Astra, who had followed her father. Would anyone, anywhere, ever want them again?

The conductor was waving to them to get back on board. It seemed they were about to set off again. After much shunting and confusion, the train reversed itself and headed back the way it had come, toward the east.

The nights on the train were long and cold. Below the seats ran heating pipes that were faintly warm, as long as the train was running. Tomas and Zigi slept behind them, under the benches; Astra and Mara lay on the floor, between them.

Tomas liked being behind the pipes; it was a kind of refuge and reminded him of the place in the woods that he'd had at home. He'd built a tiny cabin with pieces of wood and tarpaper and covered it with branches so that no one else could see it. Not even Zigi had known where his secret hideout was. He lifted his head now to look at Zigi over the backs of their two sisters. Zigi stuck out his tongue and he stuck his out in return and then Zigi made piggy eyes, pushing up his nose with his finger and pulling his eyelids down. Zigi was good at piggy eyes; they'd used to practice for hours in front of the mirror in the Jansons' parlor until Zigi's mother would come in and chase them and tell them their faces would get stuck and they'd look like pigs forever and ever. Forever and ever, amen. Say your prayers now, his mother had reminded him when he'd crawled under the seat; pray for Hugo. *Please God, keep Hugo safe and bring him back to us,* he'd gabbled inside his head. *Please*! It didn't seem too big a thing to ask for: to get your brother back. And it wasn't a selfish thing, like asking for a bicycle or a box of chocolates or a banana. He could only faintly remember what chocolates and bananas tasted like but he did know that he liked them.

Tomas could hear Astra and Mara murmuring to each other. Mara was saying, "He'll be safe somewhere, Astra, I'm sure he will." She was a comforting sort of person, Mara, always telling everyone everything would be all right. She had wide, china-blue eyes and thick brown hair woven into one fat plait, which she kept flicking over her shoulder when she trotted along beside Astra. Although only three months younger than Astra she was several inches shorter, coming up no higher than Astra's shoulder.

"He might have been trampled on in the crowd," Astra was saying.

"He's too tall, surely, to be trampled on?"

"He might have had his glasses smashed and not be able to see. That would be terrible, Mara, if he couldn't see! Just think!"

"He'd be able to see enough to follow the crowds.' .

"He might have got left behind in Gdynia and been killed in an air raid."

Tomas tried to shut his ears. He had heard it all several times already: Astra kept going over and over the various possibilities. Over and over. Until one of their parents would say, "I don't think this is helping, dear. The most likely thing is that Hugo is on another train and following us." They'd say it firmly though Tomas knew they were just saying it to quiet Astra; his mother's forehead was ridged a lot of the time like corrugated paper and his father kept chewing on his bottom lip and not hearing what people said when they spoke to him. Astra had spells of crying and spells of being angry when she'd shout at everybody and tell them that they didn't care if they never saw Hugo again. She'd accuse their father of forcing her to get on the train and not letting her wait for Hugo. Then she'd end up in her mother's arms in a torrent of weeping. And the rest of them would be sitting snuffling and rubbing their eyes with the backs of their hands and looking out of the window trying to pretend that they weren't too worried. "If we all sit and cry," said their father, "we shall be fit for nothing."

Tomas hugged Bruno to his chest and went to sleep.

He awoke with his head wedged between the two heating pipes; he had slid down during the night toward the end where they narrowed. "Help!" he croaked, but no one heard through the panting noise coming from the engine and the clattering of the wheels and the moaning of Granny Jansons and the crying of baby Klara. He wriggled and tried to get his head free but it was stuck. It might be jammed there until they got to the end of their journey—whenever that might be—and then they'd have to get someone to saw the pipes in two. Panic surged in him and he thought he was going to choke. Then he calmed himself and reached out to catch hold of Granny Jansons' ankle, which was right in front of his nose. She went leaping upward, screaming as if a rat had bitten her, but at least it brought Zigi's father down on to his hands and knees to squint underneath the seat.

"I'm stuck," squeaked Tomas.

"Hang on, young Tom! We'll get you out."

Paulis and Lukas took hold of Tomas's feet and pulled him back toward the other end where the pipes widened and there was room to slide out. Tomas felt as if his face had been put in an oven and roasted.

"Trust you, Tom!" said his father, and smiled.

After five nights they were taken off the train, near some nameless town in Poland, and herded into a camp surrounded by barbed wire. It appeared to have been an old army camp but was now swarming with refugees from the Baltic states. German sentries were on duty at the gate. German guards patrolled the perimeter.

They were allotted bunks in long, barracklike dormitories and given a couple of thin blankets each. Then they were led into another room already crowded with refugees and informed that they were to be deloused and medically examined.

"Deloused?" queried Lukas Petersons.

Yes, he was told, many refugees were covered with lice. He supposed that could be true, considering the conditions they had been living under. Paulis asked what was happening. Neither he nor anyone else in his family could understand more than a few words of German. Lukas explained.

"I have no lice," said Granny Jansons, scratching beneath

her headcovering, which started the two boys off wriggling and pretending to scratch for fleas like monkeys until their mothers reprimanded them and told them to keep still. It was important, always, they were reminded, not to draw attention to themselves.

Two white-coated women orderlies in heavy shoes came clumping in, carrying buckets full of strong-smelling disinfectant and large brushes like paintbrushes. They ordered the refugees to strip.

"What—*here*?" asked Kristina, looking around at the people in the room, both male and female. There must have been about a hundred.

"Yes, here. And loosen your hair, too. Come on, get a move on, we haven't got all day! The men first, in a line. The women sit over there, on the benches." The orderly waved toward the sides of the room which were lined with long benches.

Lukas tried to protest. "We're not animals!" He asked if at least the sexes might not be separated. But the orderlies would not listen. At the door stood two guards.

"We shall have to comply," said Lukas. "It is utterly degrading—utterly! But we have no choice. Our lives do not belong to us anymore." He began to remove his jacket.

Astra looked over at him, willing him to take back his words, wanting him to say, "No, that is not true, of course our lives belong to us!" But she knew that the days when she could run to her father for reassurance, confident that he would be able to do something to help mend a situation, were behind her, in her childhood. And yet, powerless as he might be, he was still a tower of strength. Knowing that strengthened her.

Some of the refugees who had long since accepted that they must do what they were told, and without question, were already disrobing, dropping their tattered and unkempt clothes at their feet to reveal their thin white bodies, trying to cover their private parts with their hands and preserve a little modesty.

Turning to the wall, Astra began to undress. She took her amber beads off last and laid them with her clothes on a bench, covering the necklace with her shirt. Mara placed her things alongside. She was shaking.

But Granny Jansons hugged her shawls more tightly about her and went into one of her long keenings. No one would ever take the clothes off her. No one would ever see her as naked as the day she'd been born. Her son and daughter-in-law tried to persuade her but she would not listen.

"It would be better, Mother, just to do what they say."

"Better for whom?"

One of the orderlies was coming toward them. Without a word, she began forcibly to unwind Granny Jansons from her shawls. There was nothing that Paulis and Olga could do except stand back.

"You stink!" said the orderly, wrinkling her nose. "When did you last have a bath? And you can just shut that noise off, do you hear?" She half raised a hand.

Granny fell silent, and ceasing to struggle, became limp in the woman's hands. The last of her undergarments were removed and there she stood, a bent little old woman, the sad, shriveled flesh hanging slackly on her bones. It's terrible, thought Astra. How dare they do that to Granny Jansons! She's a poor old woman who's never done anyone any harm in her life. Why should she have to go through this? Astra wanted to kick the women in white coats around and around the room like soccer balls. Glancing across at Mara, she saw that her friend was crying under her long curtain of hair. Mara's hair, released from its plait, hung to her waist. Astra wished hers did, instead of to her shoulders, so that it would cover more of her body. She crossed her arms over her chest and gripped her shoulders. She could feel goose pimples forming under her fingers.

The women sat on the benches, as ordered; the men formed two lines. They shuffled up the room, going forward one at a time to stand on small wooden boxes. The orderlies dipped their brushes into the bucket of disinfectant, swabbed their heads, which they were instructed to bend, then under their armpits and between their legs.

"Next!" they called.

When all the men had been done it was the turn of the women.

"We must preserve our dignity as best we can, Astra," said her mother. "Keep your head high. Don't let yourself feel demeaned. Remember it really does not matter—it cannot touch you, not the *real* you, the one that is inside. Come behind me."

Astra fell into line and kept her head up, following her mother's example. Many of the women were in tears. Olga was carrying the baby over her shoulder and leading Granny by the other hand.

When the moment came for Astra to step up she did so without looking at the woman in the white coat and when she felt the harsh brush on her body she did not allow herself to flinch. She stepped down and walked back up the room to collect her clothes.

Astra questioned every Latvian refugee in the camp and passed around a picture of Hugo, one of him sitting in the apple orchard under a tree with a book on his lap. He'd always had his head in a book, didn't hear half the time even when you spoke right into his ear. She had whistled and shouted, "Look at me!" and he'd glanced up and she'd snapped him, just like that, looking a bit surprised. He hadn't liked having his photograph taken.

"Sorry, dear, can't say I've seen him. But then the crowds have been so great!" And the picture would be passed back to her. It was becoming creased. She slept with it and one of Valdis beside her head every night and dreamed often of them both, sometimes happily, when they would all three be swimming in the river together, laughing and splashing, and the sun would be glittering through the trees. But in other dreams the two boys would be fighting and trying to knock each other down and then she would awake with a start and find her face wet with tears.

Every day air raid sirens wailed out, and throughout the night as well; planes were seen and heard overhead, both German and Russian; ragged-looking German army units passed in the road outside, presumably retreating; the familiar rumble of shelling and gunfire could be heard in the distance.

They were not permitted to go beyond the gates into the streets of the town. They could stand at the railings and gaze out, but that was all. They were fed regularly, usually with bread and watery cabbage soup, and left to their own devices. Families set up their own regimes, created their own spaces in the dormitories. They had no means of making divisions but it was as if invisible lines were drawn on the floor and no one transgressed them. The adults encouraged the children to play games and go out and get exercise and fresh air while they themselves—except for the sick and the elderly—strolled around the compound, exchanging news with other refugees. Rumors abounded. The Germans were on the run; the British and Americans were coming; the Germans had started a new offensive; the Russians were on the run. It was impossible to find out anything definite. If

Lukas asked questions he was treated with looks of suspicion. The atmosphere encircling the camp was fraught with tension—no doubt because of the proximity of the Russian front.

One morning the Gestapo arrived. The clump of jackboots could be heard as they went from hut to hut. The refugees were quiet, even the small children. The very word Gestapo was enough to send a ripple of fear through the whole complex.

When an officer pushed open the door of their dormitory everyone froze, as if playing the game of statues. Astra felt a shiver run up her spine. The man standing in the doorway looked so hard, with his glinting knee-length boots, his swastika armband, and his ice-cold eyes. He was looking at them as if they were vermin.

"Heil Hitler!" He brought his arm up in the Nazi salute.

One after the other, the arms rose. Lukas's was the last to move. The Gestapo officer noticed it. Another shiver went shooting up Astra's spine and made her head twitch. Her father hated the Nazis just as he hated the Communists, but she wished that he didn't have to let it show so openly in his face. She saw that her mother's face was ashy pale and small bands of sweat were standing out around her hairline.

The German pursed his lips, then began to stroll between the lines of bunks, his merciless eyes noting their bedrolls and pots and pans and clothes hung to dry on pieces of string. From each family he demanded papers. He has the power to do with us anything that he wants to do, thought Astra. He could decide we are spies and have us sent off to wherever it is that they send the Jews. Her father said that no one knew for certain where the Jews were taken but he suspected that many would not return. He did not expect to see his old friend Oscar again.

The man from the Gestapo had reached them. He held out his hand. Lukas and Paulis produced their papers.

"So you are all Latvian here? We liberated you from the Russians, did we not?" He stared Lukas in the eye.

Astra was on tenterhooks. Her father was not answering right away. Surely he was not going to say, "Liberated us? Well, yes, I suppose you did, but then you stayed and occupied us and did not give us back to ourselves. We would like to belong to ourselves, to be an independent nation again." She knew that that was what her father would be thinking but of course he would not speak his thoughts aloud, he was not rash enough for that. And she was being idiotic to imagine that he might. The palms of her hands were soaking wet. She wiped them on her skirt.

"Indeed," said Lukas, nodding, returning the officer's stare, "that is true."

The German studied the papers, checked the heads in the circle.

"One is missing?"

"My son Hugo."

"Where is he?"

"We do not know. We got separated from him in Gdynia."

Wherever Hugo is, thought Astra, he will be without papers. An illegal immigrant. And if the Gestapo were to encounter him they might well put him in prison.

The next morning, Pastor Vizulis came to tell them that they were about to be moved on again. The camp was going to be needed for soldiers returning wounded from the front and, as they could see for themselves, their numbers were increasing daily.

Before lunchtime they were back on a train and traveling

westward once more to yet another unknown destination. They only knew that they were going west by the position of the sun. Listening to the *clickety-click* of the wheels turning beneath her, Astra felt somewhere deep inside herself that they were going in the right direction to find Hugo. As they'd journeyed east she had felt uneasy, had had the sensation of going farther and farther away from him. As they approached the German border, her spirit lightened.

Their next camp, near Hanover in the northwest of the country, had been a Russian prisoner-of-war barrack. It was heavily ringed with barbed wire and guarded by German soldiers. There was also a barbed-wire division up the middle, and on the other side were internees, foreign nationals whose countries were fighting against Germany and who had been trapped here at the outbreak of war. Lukas talked through the wire to some Belgian priests. They looked emaciated and their eyes were sunken. Would the war be over soon, they wanted to know. Perhaps, said Lukas; hard facts were difficult to come by. The priests had heard that the Americans had crossed the German frontier and were fighting in the Rühr and Saar valleys.

Within an hour of arriving at the camp, Astra had ascertained that Hugo was not there. She searched every hut. More people arrived in the following days but he was not among them.

"I feel as if my right arm has been chopped off," she told Mara as they paced around the camp together. They walked for hours, around and around, and Astra watched the road outside, in case a truck should draw up and disgorge another load of refugees. "Sometimes I think I will have to run away and look for him myself."

"You mustn't do that," said Mara, alarmed. "Promise me that you will not?" She knew her friend to be headstrong and impetuous, whereas Hugo, the perfect complement for her, was slower to act and more cautious. It was strange that it was Hugo who should be missing. If it had been Astra they would have said, "What is she up to, that girl? Whom has she stopped to talk to?"

"Promise, Astra!" pleaded Mara.

"Oh, all right! Where could I start, anyway?"

They passed the guard known as Tempo. He had a wooden leg and hobbled at great rate around the compound shouting, "Tempo, Tempo!"—"Quickly, quickly!"—impatient with anyone like Granny Jansons who moved too slowly for his liking. He said that Germany was winning the war, it was all lies to say they were retreating. No one did say it publicly: defeatist talk could lead to imprisonment. "The Fatherland will never be defeated!" Tempo declared, raising his arm up toward the sky, which was clotted with gray, elephantine barrage balloons. In spite of them, British and American bombers were overhead at regular intervals, releasing their deadly cargoes.

The light was failing, the days were short. It was now the month of December. The girls turned to go back to their quarters, a garage at the rear of the camp. Although it was miserably cold and floored in stone, they preferred it to the long, crowded barrack.

As they crossed the yard, they met Lukas, who had been to see the camp commandant.

"Did you ask him—can we get permits to travel to Leipzig?" asked Astra eagerly.

"I think there's a good chance. This place is crammed and they're desperate to get rid of people. And we do have somewhere to go. I showed him Otto's letter."

For days they kept their fingers crossed, without letting their hopes rise too high. To get away from these awful camps with their barbed wire and hordes of dejected people and live in a house with friends—was that not too much to hope for?

A week later, Lukas was summoned to the commandant's office. Travel permits for both families had come through, along with civilian ration books. Without either, they could not have moved.

"But can we all go?" asked Olga. "Are you sure that it is all right for us to come, too, Mrs. Petersons? There are so many of us."

"Of course you must come, Olga. We wouldn't consider leaving you behind. We are all in this together and we are not going to be parted. At the very least, Otto will have a garage for us, or a shed!"

They arrived in Leipzig on Christmas Eve after another long, slow train journey. The city had taken a heavy toll in bombing raids. Some streets had been blitzed to the ground. German soldiers—young, mostly—shuffled about in various states of disability, hobbling stiff-legged on crutches, splinted arms sticking out from their bodies at odd angles. Medals dangled forlornly from their chests. Their eyes, when they raised them, reflected pain and dejection.

Shouldering their burdens, the two families set out from the railway station to find a bus that would take them to Professor Zimmermann's street. Lukas asked for directions. On the way to the bus stop they passed the famous fifteenth-century church of St. Thomas.

"Look, children!" Lukas halted them in front of it. "That is where the great Bach was music master."

They gazed up at its tower and soaring roof.

"Bach wrote the St. Matthew Passion for St. Thomas's," said Kristina.

"Professor Zimmermann sent Hugo a postcard of the church once," said Astra. "I remember it!"

While they stood they heard organ music welling up inside the church. "Bach." Kristina smiled. They listened closely. Then voices rose to mingle with the strains of the organ. "Sounds like one of his cantatas," said Kristina. "What a treat!"

"It's a pity we can't go in," said Astra wistfully.

"There isn't time, I'm afraid," said Lukas. "We must get to the Zimmermanns' before dark."

Astra lingered a moment, and had to run to catch up to the others.

At the bus stop they waited for almost an hour, crowding close together for protection from the cutting wind. At last a bus came and took them on the last lap of their journey to the suburb where the Zimmermanns lived.

They found the house easily. It was large, with wide casement windows and overhanging eaves, and it even had a big spreading fir tree in the front garden.

"A Christmas tree!" cried Tomas. "See, Zig!"

"It looks like a lovely house," said Mara shyly.

They stayed on the pavement while Lukas went up the path to the front door. He knocked and stepped back to wait. It was growing steadily colder, the day was waning fast. Granny Jansons was complaining again and Klara was hungry. The boys stamped their feet to keep them warm and hugged their hands under their armpits. Then Tomas touched Zigi on the arm and cried, "Can't catch me!" and ran. Zigi pursued hotly. Their rucksacks bobbed up and down on their backs. Tomas ducked up the path and swerved across the grass to dodge behind the fir tree.

"Come back!" called Kristina in a low, commanding voice. They came at once, looking sheepish. "We don't want them to think we're an unruly lot! And do up your rucksack, Tom—you're going to drop something out of it if you're not careful."

Her attention was diverted by the door of the house opening. An elderly woman swaddled in shawls shuffled out onto the step. Was it Frau Zimmermann? They had never seen her. She had not accompanied her husband on his trips to Latvia. Her head was hunched over. She raised it to look up the path past Lukas to where the rest of them stood bunched together.

"Some of us should have waited around the corner," murmured Astra, "and appeared at the last moment." Glancing up at the top windows, she saw the faces of two boys. So there were children in the house already. Grandchildren of the Zimmermanns perhaps? They looked about the same age as their boys, maybe a little younger.

Lukas and the woman talked, for several minutes. The low murmur of their voices floated up the path to them though they could not hear what they said. A few spots of rain touched their cheeks. Tomas was leaning against his mother's back. Astra wished she could do the same. She was so tired. Lukas and the woman were still talking. Astra kept her eyes fastened on her, willing her to invite them in, and quickly. They could talk later.

But the woman was turning away and putting her back to Lukas! And now she was going inside and the door was closing. It wasn't possible! She *must* let them come in, even for a little while. They watched, stunned, as Lukas retraced his steps down the path, his own head bowed, now.

"What's wrong, Father?" Astra was first to speak.

"Otto died three months ago. Of pleurisy. And I'm afraid his widow doesn't want to know us."

"It wasn't because I ran around the tree, was it?" asked Tomas.

6

A SIGNALMAN returning home along the railway track stumbled over Hugo's feet. He swung his masked lantern up the length of the boy's body until it rested on the face. In the feeble light the skin appeared the color of pale mud. The eyes were closed. He looked as still as death.

Setting down the lantern, Herr Schneider knelt and brought his face close to the boy's. It had the chill of death on it, too, and showed no flicker of reaction. Herr Schneider placed his hand over the lips. There seemed to be a slight sensation of warmth. He thrust his hand into the boy's sodden jacket and felt for the heart. There was a beat, but it was very faint, little more than a flutter. He tried to raise the boy but he was a dead weight and his head flopped backward.

Herr Schneider picked up the lantern and ran the half mile to his cottage. His wife and daughter were sitting by the kitchen stove, winding wool that they had ripped from old jerseys and washed and dried. His wife was holding the ball and Bettina the skeins between her raised hands. They turned to look at him, surprised by the abruptness of his entrance. Their faces were flushed from the heat of the stove.

"Quickly, Grete, Bettina! Put on your coats and come with me! There is a boy lying down by the railway track and he is near to death."

Bettina and her mother dropped the wool, stamped their feet into rubber boots, and tugged on their coats. Frau Schneider wrapped a scarf around her head. Herr Schneider had already set out back along the track to the railway line. They followed the bobbing glimmer of light. The wind, suddenly turning fierce, tore at their coats and whipped Bettina's unrestrained hair across her face. The rain, which earlier had been torrenting down, had ceased, but low, heavy clouds were keeping the sky dark.

They climbed the fence and slid down the embankment. Mud oozed around their boots. Bettina put out a hand to steady her mother. Her father was holding the lantern aloft so that they could see the boy and the way that he lay. His head was angled to one side, chin tilted down toward the shoulder, and the body looked slack, like a broken marionette.

"You take the lantern, Grete. Bettina, can you manage his legs if I take his shoulders?"

"Has he been hit by a train?" asked Frau Schneider. "He might have broken bones."

"We'll carry him as gently as we can."

Herr Schneider squatted behind the boy and slid his hands down under his shoulders until they gripped the sides of his chest. Bettina took hold of his knees.

"Ready?"

"Yes."

"Now!"

Together they raised Hugo from the ground. His body felt thin and bony, but in his unconscious state he was leaden and heavy. His booted feet dangled, bumping against Bettina's thighs.

"Be careful, Gustav," said Frau Schneider anxiously, for her husband had a heart condition. It was the reason that he had not been conscripted into the army. You are lucky, her sister had said; her husband had been killed on the Russian front. There were several war widows in the area, as well as parents who had lost sons. The Klingers, who kept the village shop, had lost two sons. In the shop window they had pictures of the boys draped in black crêpe. *For the glory of the Fatherland,* Herr Klinger had written in large black letters on a placard beneath. Herr Schneider said to talk of glory in war was stupid and his wife had to hush him and tell him to watch what he said. You never knew who would report you to the Gestapo. They had eyes and ears everywhere and were quick to act on information against anyone who spoke critically of the regime. Herr Schneider's brother in Berlin had been reported for criticizing Hitler for invading Poland and had been arrested. He was still imprisoned.

Frau Schneider did feel lucky that she had not had to sacrifice any of her family, but she was still anxious when Gustav lifted heavy weights or pushed himself too far. He was not a man to give up easily. She could hear the wheeze of his breath as he and Bettina labored with their burden, slipping and sliding on the greasy bank. Frau Schneider set down the lantern to help them lift the boy over the fence.

"Rest a moment, Gustav."

"I cannot, Grete. He has little time left. I am fine, don't worry! It will be easier now that we are on level ground." Herr Schneider took a deep breath then moved off again, walking backward into the wind, with Hugo's head lolling against his stomach. Bettina struggled to keep his legs up as high as she could. Her back and shoulders ached.

They reached the cottage and carried the boy in. They laid him in front of the stove. Could he still be alive, wondered Bettina, seeing the pallor of his face under the light. Her mother had already gone down on her knees and was stripping off his wet clothes. Bettina fetched a goose-feather quilt from the box bed to wrap him in, and they placed a pillow under his head. Frau Schneider gently chafed his blue hands and feet. They thought they could see very slight signs of color creeping into his gray cheeks. Black blood was caked on his brow and down the side of his right ear.

"He has a bad head wound there, by the looks of it," said Herr Schneider. "We will have to fetch Doctor Braun."

"I'll go, Father." Bettina jumped up. "You stay here."

Lifting the lantern, she went back out into the stormy night. She took a short cut to the village, along the edge of the wood, which normally she did not use after dark. But this was not a normal night. As she ducked her head under dripping, overhanging branches, her feet squelching on the path, she thought about the boy and realized that he might die before she could return with Doctor Braun. So many people whom they had known had died. She shivered as a splatter of cold raindrops driven by the wind struck her face. The gnarled branches of the trees looked like the twisted limbs of witches. Some low ones snatched at her hair. She pushed them back and pressed on.

She was glad to leave the wood behind and enter the village, even though no lights showed at the cottage windows except for some small chinks here and there where the blackout curtains did not meet exactly. There was one at the window of her friend Hilde's house and she was tempted to rap on the door and go in for a moment to tell Hilde what had happened. But time was too precious.

The doctor lived in the biggest house, at the far end of the village. Bettina trudged up the driveway and banged the heavy brass knocker hard on the stout oak door. They were elderly, the Brauns, and hard of hearing, and they seldom invited anyone to cross the doorstep of their home. Doctor

Braun consulted in a small wooden building at the side of the house. He had given up working some years before but had had to come out of retirement because of the war; the younger doctors had been sent off to the front. Bettina banged again.

At last she heard shuffling feet and a chain rattling behind the door, which was then opened a few inches. Through the narrow slit she saw one half of Frau Braun's face. The eye was squinting as it tried to focus.

"Who is that?"

"Bettina Schneider. Signalman Schneider's daughter. We need Herr Doctor Braun to come—"

"He is not here. He is at the military hospital."

"When will he be back?"

"I do not know. It is impossible to tell. I am sorry." The door closed.

Wearily Bettina returned home.

"We will just have to nurse him ourselves," said her mother.

In the shop next morning Bettina was questioned by Herr Klinger while he weighed out their sugar ration. "So, I hear you have a lodger?" He looked up into her face. He was looking at her with suspicion, she thought. He and his wife were suspicious people, forever poking and prying and asking questions; they always had been, even before the war started. And they were friendly with the local Gestapo.

Bettina hated to come into the shop but had no choice; it was the only one in the village. She felt sorry for the Klingers because they had lost their sons, but she hated the way they went on about Hitler and Germany ruling the world. Her own father was a peaceful man, a pacifist, against war; who thought that countries should get on with running themselves and looking after their people and never mind trying to conquer the world. For what? What good would it do anyone except make those in power feel more powerful? It was not for the benefit of the people, most of whom wished to lead quiet, uneventful lives in their own homes. He had warned his daughter, though, not to repeat any of these things outside their own home.

"Who is he, then, this boy you have taken in?" Herr Klinger's voice was insistent.

"We do not know. A refugee, Father thinks."

Herr Klinger pursed his lips.

Later that day, a policeman came roaring up the lane on his motorcycle and stopped outside their cottage.

"Mother—it's the police!" Bettina shrank back from the window. Her father was at work.

"Don't worry, love! It is not the Gestapo." Frau Schneider wiped her hands on her apron and went to open the door. Bettina stood in front of the box bed in which the boy lay, unconscious.

The policeman stepped into the kitchen and looked around. He said he had heard they were harboring a stranger.

"My husband was coming to the police station today after work to report the matter," said Frau Schneider. She looked toward the box bed and Bettina moved aside so that the policeman could approach.

He bent over and touched the boy's face. "Seems to be alive, though only just. Who is he?"

"We don't know. We found him by the railway track. He has no papers, nothing."

"He looks too young to be a soldier."

"I think he might be about fourteen years old," said Frau Schneider, choosing her words carefully, knowing that at sixteen boys were being taken into the military. Not that this boy would make much of a soldier for a long time to come.

"He could be a refugee. There are some billeted at the summer camp."

"Perhaps his family might be there?"

"I'll make inquiries."

The policeman came back two days later to say that the refugees had been moved on, nobody knew where. "We'll let the boy stay with you in the meantime and if he lives we'll decide what to do with him then."

"He would certainly die if he were to be moved now," said Frau Schneider.

The policeman nodded. "He's not a Jew, anyway," he said, moving toward the door. "There were no Jews among those refugees." He went out. They listened to the *phut-phut* of his motor bike dying away.

"Would he have taken him away if he had been a Jew?" asked Bettina.

"I suppose so." Her mother sighed. "It's terrible, all the things that are happening." She spoke very quietly, scarcely above a whisper, and with one eye on the window, in case the policeman should come back.

"Can't *anyone* do *anything* about it?"

"Not now. Your father says that perhaps earlier, in the thirties, when the Nazis were coming to power, something might have been done. But you've seen the Gestapo, Bettina! What could we do if they were to come to our door one night to take this boy away?"

For days, which then ran into weeks, their patient hung between life and death. On the day after they had found him he developed a high fever and color surged back into his body. His cheeks looked cherry-red as if they had been rouged, his forehead was hot and dry, and his chest was racked with harsh coughing that left him gasping. Pneumonia, thought Frau Schneider, and no wonder with the soaking he had had! They steamed kettles to help him breathe, sponged his body, dressed his head wound, which continued to gape and suppurate, fed him liquids, and watched over him day and night, taking shifts, the three of them. They kept him in the box bed in the kitchen, the warmest room in the house, the place where they cooked and ate and lived, going only into the two small cold back rooms at night to sleep. The stove in the kitchen was never allowed to die down; the nearby wood provided ample kindling.

From time to time the boy opened his eyes and looked about, but he did not seem to register anything, and when delirious he babbled in a tongue they did not know. It was a strange tongue, unlike any they had ever heard. They did not know anything about him, not his name or his country or whether he had any kin. The only things that he had had in his pockets were a plain white linen handkerchief of good quality, monogrammed with the letter H, a bandage, and a small box that had disintegrated with the wet, but seemed to have contained some kind of white tablets. Herr Schneider presumed these must have been medication of some sort.

Doctor Braun called one day but said there was nothing more that he could do for their patient than what they were already doing. It was too late to stitch the head wound; there was bound to be a scar.

"Keep him warm, nourish him as much as you can, and allow him to rest. Then you must hope for the best. He should be in the hospital but there are no beds available." He shrugged. He was very stooped these days, Frau Schneider observed after he had gone.

"He looks haunted. He has seen too much, I expect."

At school, Bettina talked about the boy to her friend Hilde.

"Are you sure he's not a spy?" asked Hilde. He could be

Russian or British, for all you know. They say the British are dropping lots of spies behind our lines and we should be on the lookout for them."

"He is not a spy," said Bettina hotly. "He's not old enough for one thing. And he is not British—I *do* know some English words!"

Hilde looked at her in surprise. Bettina was known to have an even temper and to be difficult to rile. She went home with her to see the boy for herself.

They pulled back the curtains of the box bed and leaned over him.

"What age do you think he is?" whispered Hilde.

"About our age, Mother thinks." They were soon to be fifteen, Hilde at the end of December, Bettina early in January.

"He would be quite handsome if he were not so thin."

At that moment he opened his eyes and they blushed and drew back.

"Astra?" he said, frowning.

"Who is Astra?" asked Bettina, but he had closed his eyes again and sunk back down into the twilight place where he dwelled beyond their reach.

Surfacing from time to time into consciousness, Hugo became aware, little by little, of his surroundings and of the people who tended him. Everything and everyone he saw was blurred, with fuzzy edges, as if ringed with light. He came to recognize first the inside of the cupboardlike place in which he lay; it was lined with planks of yellowish-brown wood and encompassed him on three sides. He stared for long spells at the wood, trying to fathom the flecks on it, trying to identify them. Were they knots? Words slipped from the edge of his mind. Mists still swirled in his head, clouding it.

The open side of the cupboard framed a room. By concentrating, he gradually brought the pieces of furniture into focus—not into sharp relief, but they became sufficiently clear for him to be able to know what they were, even if he could not always put a name to them. There was a dark brown object broken by circles of blue and white—plates?—and a big, square, white wooden table in the middle of the room and three deep chairs with arms drawn up before the stove. Sometimes the door of the stove would be open and he could see the fire. It held his eyes spellbound, flickering and crackling, changing color, now burning fiercely, now dying down; then, with a new log thrown upon it, sparking again and leaping upward into the chimney like a live thing.

And then there were the people. The man had broad shoulders and firm, gentle hands that held him while he drank. His thick brown hair was brushed straight back from his forehead and his mustache was bushy and brown also. The woman had blond hair braided around her head, and often she smiled as she bent over him and her lips would move and make sounds that he could not decipher. The girl was blond, too, with brighter hair than the woman's—sunshine-yellow it was and it curled all over her head—and she had pink cheeks. He had a feeling that her eyes would be the color of cornflowers. Sometimes he heard laughter in the room and knew she was there. He recognized all these sights and sounds as the mist in his head rolled slowly away.

He began, also, to recognize words.

"Drink this," said the woman and he drank from a cup. It was warm milk sweetened with honey. The taste brought back to him the memory of another room in another place and another woman with fair hair knotted at the back of her neck saying "Drink this" and giving him milk and honey. But the two women had not spoken in the same language.

"Are you feeling better today?" asked the woman with the braided blond hair.

"*Danke,*" he said.

"So you understand German?" She smiled.

He nodded. He seemed to understand.

"What is your language?"

His head hurt with trying to think. The fog was closing in again. He was tired. He closed his eyes and allowed himself to drift into sleep.

Wakening, later, when the curtains were closed and the lamp lit, he heard them talking. They sounded excited.

"He spoke to me this morning! He said '*Danke*'!"

"He must be coming around."

"Perhaps he is German, after all."

"No, I think not. Remember that when he was delirious he did not speak German."

The man and the woman were sitting on either side of the stove. Where was the girl? He let his eyes swivel. She was standing by the window, reaching up with her arms to put strands of color onto the branches of a small tree. A fir tree? He could smell pine needles and the smell took him back to another memory, in that other place. This time he could see more of it: not only a room but the house itself with a long verandah and an apple-green door and a funny old weathercock on the rooftop, and behind the house a wood of birch and fir trees that spread up onto the hill. He knew that place well. It was his home!

He could hear a girl singing. *Stille Nacht, heilige Nacht. . . .* Silent night, holy night. . . . He smiled. It must be Christmas.

"He's awake, Mother!"

The girl left the tree and came to his bedside. She kneeled

down so that her face was level with his. Her hair shone like a sunflower around her head.

"Can you hear me?" she asked softly.

He nodded.

"What is your name? And where are you from?"

"My name is Hugo Petersons," he said clearly. "And I am from Latvia."

7

THE PETERSONS and Jansons spent Christmas Eve in the railway station at Leipzig.

"We cannot really blame Frau Zimmermann," said Lukas. "She already has two refugee families billeted with her—one family is from Estonia—and her health is not good. She feels she has enough on her hands."

"So it's not because I ran around the tree?" asked Tomas anxiously.

"No, Tom." His mother smiled. "And next year we'll have a good Christmas, you'll see!" she said and led them in the singing of carols, the way she used to do back home, with them all standing around the piano and the white candles on the Christmas tree flickering. The station lamps were harsh and cast a gloomy light.

Silent night, holy night. . . . Astra's voice wavered. The night was not in the least bit silent, with people coming and going and milling about, and she did not know how holy it could be, either, with all the awful things that were going on. She could not get Hugo out of her mind. If only she knew where he was and if he was all right. It was the not knowing anything—the total blank—that was so difficult to cope with. It was as if Hugo had dropped from sight, behind a curtain. She wondered at her mother's firm, strong voice, which could be heard soaring above everyone else's. Yet her mother must be wondering, as she was, what now? Where could they go? Back to a camp with barbed wire and guards to sleep fifty, sixty to a room? But even that would be better than a railway platform. Other refugees had gathered around and were joining in the carols. Their singing was fervent, almost prayerful. *Sleep in heavenly peace. . . .*

When they were settling down in a waiting room to sleep as best they could, Tomas opened his rucksack to find that his teddy bear was missing.

"Bruno's not here!" He rummaged through socks and underpants, jerseys, glass marbles, a book of Hans Christian Andersen's *Fairy Tales,* a fishing line and float, colored pencils, pieces of paper—he went right to the bottom of the sack. Then he tipped out the contents and rifled through them again. His mother and Astra helped, although they could see at a glance that the bear was not there. "He's lost—Bruno's lost!" wailed Tomas. "It's not fair!" Tears welled up in his eyes. He had had Bruno since his first birthday.

The bear must have dropped out of the rucksack at the Zimmermanns', they decided, when Tomas had been playing tag with Zigi.

"I'm sorry, love," said Kristina, "but there's nothing we can do."

Zigi gave him his best red marble, which Tomas had been coveting for months.

"Thanks, Zig." Tomas clutched it in his hand. It was nice of Zigi. Not that a marble could ever make up for Bruno!

In the morning, cramped and stiff—a morning condition they were well accustomed to—they set off for a school which they'd been told was being used to house refugees. It was a miserably cold, bleak place, with long corridors which the wind shrieked through, and it smelled of chalk and ink and acrid disinfectant. There were only hard seats and desks to sit or lie on. They were so exhausted they slept sprawled on benches.

"Tomorrow, Paulis and I will go into the country," said Lukas, "and see if we can find somewhere else to stay. We must try to get out of the city." In wars, cities were dangerous places.

The men were away all day. Tomas and Zigi played in the playground with some other boys, one of whom produced a soccer ball, soggy and dented, but a ball, nevertheless, that could be kicked and thrown and wrestled for. Their shouts echoed around the yard. Astra and Mara, wishing they could let off steam in that way, recommenced their promenading, going out into the suburban streets. As usual, Hugo provided the main topic for their conversation. Valdis had dropped back in Astra's memory, had become a boy with whom she had swum in the river in summertime. Would it ever be summer again?

"Sometimes I get the feeling that Hugo is dead," said Astra. "There is a kind of blackness that covers my heart."

Mara burst into tears. "Don't say that, Astra! It's a dreadful thing to say. If you think it, you might make it come about." Mara was inclined to be superstitious, would never walk on cracks on the pavement, avoided number thirteen as if it were a plague. Astra, in defiance of fate, would walk on cracks and maintained that thirteen was her lucky number.

"If anything does happen to Hugo, you can't blame me!" Astra spoke sharply. She moved away from Mara a little. She felt not only angry but also quite aggressive toward Mara without fully understanding why. Her friend had covered her face with her hands and was sobbing behind them. Her shoulders were shaking, her brown head bobbing up and down. Astra frowned. She broke a piece of twig from a garden hedge and snapped it in two between her fingers. She glanced sideways at Mara. A suspicion was beginning to form in her head. "Don't tell me you're sweet on Hugo!"

Mara dropped her hands and looked up. She was blushing and crying at the same time.

"You *are*!" said Astra accusingly.

Mara sniffed and tossed her plait over her shoulder. Her lip trembled. "What if I am? Why shouldn't I be?"

The two girls stared at each other, then Astra veered abruptly to the right, crossed the road, and walked off.

She walked for miles, around this strange, unknown city, the adrenaline running in her system, restoring her energy. She scarcely noticed the ruins or the long lines outside shops or the army tanks and trucks as they hurtled by or the groups of wounded soldiers standing on street corners or the procession of Hitler Jugend beating drums. She walked like an automaton. She did not think of anything. She allowed her mind to go blank.

And then she stopped dead. In front of her was the church of St. Thomas. She went inside.

The interior was dim and quiet except for the sound of the organ. When her eyes had adjusted she slipped into a pew near the back. The stained-glass windows seemed to glow around her. There was a smell of old stone, of antiquity. She leaned back and closed her eyes and listened to the music. It was Bach again, that much she could tell. A fugue, she thought. Her mother would have known. She felt the music calming, quietening her. She let out a long sigh. She thought of all the people who must have come here over the centuries. And it was still standing—the bombs had not got it.

She thought of Hugo. She prayed for Hugo.

Refreshed, and more at peace, she returned to the city's war-scarred streets. She must get back to the others quickly, night was closing in, her parents would be worrying. After she had walked for ten minutes she realized that she was lost, had no idea in which direction she should go. Panic gripped her. Her eyes began to mist over, her heart to race and thump. Every corner looked the same. The streets had grown dark and were full of shadows. Men called out to her. She ran past them. She approached several women. A school? they repeated. Which school? A big, high gloomy brick building with a yard in front. She did not know its name. Using her hands, she tried to show its size and shape. Which district? She did not know the district. In the end she stumbled upon the street by chance—by luck. It was pitch dark. She was exhausted now.

Her mother was standing on the pavement.

"Astra, where have you been? I've been worried sick about you!"

"I lost my way."

"Don't ever go off like that on your own again, do you hear me?"

For a moment Astra thought her mother might strike her. She had never struck her. She must have thought she'd got lost, properly lost, like Hugo. She put her arm around her mother. "I didn't mean to worry you, Mama, I'm sorry!" Now they were both crying, locked together, holding each other tightly.

"It's not easy for any of us," said her mother, drying her eyes and lifting her head. She always carried her head very proudly, and every morning brushed her hair till it shone before twisting it into its knot. "We're all on short fuses."

Astra nodded. That was exactly how she felt, and if someone were to strike a spark nearby she was sure a flame would lick right through her and set her alight.

"And what did you do to poor Mara? She was in a terrible state when she came in."

"I was nasty to her, I'm afraid." Astra sighed. "I hadn't realized she was carrying a candle for Hugo."

"You were jealous?"

"I suppose," admitted Astra reluctantly.

"But you don't own him, you know, dear, even though you are his twin. You mustn't be too possessive about him."

"How can I be possessive?" cried Astra. "When he's lost to us?"

"Let's hope not forever," said her mother quietly. "Now go and find Mara and make amends. I know you're not particularly good at saying sorry in situations like this, but you'll just have to work at it. You can be too proud, Astra. You must try also to be generous."

Astra opened her mouth to make a retort, then closed it again. She knew her mother to be right.

She found Mara sitting at a desk in one of the classrooms. She was reading. When she saw Astra coming she flipped her plait over her shoulder and turned her head.

"I'm sorry, Mara," Astra mumbled to her back. "I was horrible to you. And I don't mind if you are fond of Hugo." She swallowed, then added, "I'm sure he's fond of you, too."

Mara looked around. She was always quick to make up, was not one to hold a grudge. "That's all right, Astra, I understand," she said, and getting up, she held out her hands and Astra took them and squeezed them and they laughed together. They were best friends again, although Astra knew—as did Mara—that in the future, when they talked of Hugo, they would talk as if they shared him, as if Mara had a right to part of him. Astra knew, too, that it would take some time for her to get used to that idea.

It was late in the evening when their fathers returned. They were weary. Lukas was limping badly.

"Did you find any place for us?" asked Olga.

Paulis shook his head. "We tried a lot of farms—some had refugees already, others said they were short of food."

"We'll go out again tomorrow," said Lukas.

The men pulled off their shoes and socks to reveal blisters as big as pebbles on their feet.

"You can't walk on feet like that," Kristina objected.

"We'll have to."

"Can't Mara and I go with you?" Astra suggested, but her father said they should stay at home and help their mothers and save their shoe leather.

Lukas and Paulis went out every day and came back every evening to tell the same story. It seemed hopeless. More refugees poured into the school. The place smelled of sour, unwashed bodies now, as well as disinfectant. Poor, inadequate food was dished out twice daily. Children became ill with colds and influenza, scarlet fever, dysentry. Some were taken to the hospital. Most of the elderly had stomach complaints. The nights were freezing cold and noisy with the sound of hacking coughs, crying and groaning, and air raid sirens. When the sirens wailed, they crawled under the heavy wooden desks, held their breath, and prayed.

Astra snuggled up close to Mara, who slept deeply through all commotions. Astra could hear her own stomach rumbling. It felt bloated and full of wind. She was *so* hungry. She could never remember feeling so hungry in her life before. Sometimes when she'd been out in the fresh air for a long time playing tennis or volleyball she'd come in and say, "I'm starving!" But it had been nothing compared to this. She sucked the back of her hand and tried to think of lazy summer days at home before the war, when she was a small child. The sounds had all been soft and low and unhurried.

The whirr of insects, the drone of bees, the mooing of Klavins' cows, the plop of a tennis ball as it met a racket. . . . It usually helped her to drift off.

One morning, when their fathers were too exhausted to go out, Astra proposed that she and Mara go instead. Lukas had to be persuaded.

"We'll be all right! We'll be careful, won't we, Mara? And we'll be back before dark."

Lukas told them an area to try, southwest of the city, toward the town of Gera, and gave them some money.

The girls managed to find a bus, which took them to the outskirts of the city, and then a mail van gave them a lift a short way. After that they walked. The wind was bitter. They pulled their woolen caps well down over their ears and linked arms. The roads up to the farms were long and rutted. Ice had formed in the tracks left by tractor wheels. Farmyard dogs snapped at their heels. Geese chased them. Doors were closed in their faces. One or two opened and they were invited in for hot drinks by the fire.

As light was leaving the land and they thought to turn homeward, they knocked on a door and were invited in by the farmer's wife, Frau Mann. She had a red, cheerful face and was sympathetic.

"You poor girls! You look frozen. Take some of this soup and bring your chairs in close to the fire. I shall ask my husband if he will let you lodge in our barn. He could do with help around the farm—all the men are away at the front."

Farmer Mann came back with her and said that yes, he could use some help. Were the men strong? he wanted to know. Very strong, said Astra, thinking of her father's leg. But they could all help, she and Mara, too, and even the boys.

"We'd be *most* grateful, Herr Mann." She looked up at him, appealing to him, begging him.

"Very well. We'll give it a try. But there's only the barn to sleep in."

They did not mind that—anything to get away from the school and Leipzig.

It was evening by the time they made it back to the city, but their parents neglected to scold them when they heard their news.

"You've done well, girls!" said Lukas.

"Think how nice it will be to have green fields around us again!" Kristina turned to Mara's mother. "Won't it, Olga?"

"It will be wonderful, Mrs. Petersons!" Olga's eyes were shining. She hated towns and cities. Before they'd set out on this journey she had never spent a night in one.

"Do you know, Olga, I think it is time you stopped calling me Mrs. Petersons! We have been through a great deal together, and we are living as one family, so I would like you to call me Kristina from now on. And you, too, Paulis."

"That goes for me as well," said Lukas.

Olga blushed.

"Thank you," said Paulis and then added, somewhat self-consciously, "Lukas."

They all smiled.

Before they moved to the farm, Lukas went back to the Zimmermanns' to leave a note for Hugo telling him where they were going.

"Look for Bruno, please, Papa!" pleaded Tomas.

Keeping his promise, Lukas walked around the fir tree before knocking on the Zimmermanns' door, but there was no sign of Tomas's one-eyed bear. It could easily have dropped out somewhere else. Or maybe one of the children in the house had picked it up. He could hardly expect Frau Zimmermann to question them for him. He was afraid that Tomas was just going to have to do without his bear.

Frau Zimmermann, when she answered his knock, said that she would keep the note safe for Hugo.

"I am sorry, you know," she mumbled, not looking Lukas in the face.

"It's all right, Frau Zimmermann, I understand. I realize you have had enough to cope with."

The barn was roomy and high and they had dry straw to sleep on and the animals below sent up their heat.

"I never thought I'd see the day when I'd be sleeping above cows!" said Granny Jansons, but her grumble was only halfhearted. After the chilly school with its harsh surfaces and sharp edges, and the corridors ringing with the sound of feet, straw and animals, soft grass and the lowing of cattle soothed them.

Frau Mann gave them a few odds and ends of furniture, quilts, and kitchen utensils. Kristina and Olga made a little kitchen in a shed close by, safely away from the straw. They had a spirit stove which would hold one pot at a time and a basin for washing the pots and dishes in. There was not much to cook except turnips and potatoes—mostly potatoes—and an occasional egg. They lived on that, and bread and milk.

Olga, though, found a way to earn some extra food: she told fortunes and was rewarded with eggs and small packets of sugar and tea. She had a flair, and her fame soon spread.

A woman came one day to ask if Olga could tell her whether her husband was alive or dead. He was away at the front and there had been no news of him for a long time.

Olga carried a basin of water up from the yard and placed it in front of a mirror so that the water would be reflected.

Next, she lit two candles. Their light flickered over the silvery glass. The woman waited with her hands clasped together. Olga told her to drop her wedding ring into the water and then to look at the mirror. The woman did so. She sat silent, her face impassive. Suddenly, she cried out.

"I can see him! I can see my Dieter! And he has a mustache. He has never had a mustache before."

The following day, the woman's husband came home, on crutches, and sporting a mustache! From then on, women from all around flocked to the Manns' barn to consult Olga. "I cannot promise results," she told them, "but you may try if you wish." They did wish. Some saw their husbands, some did not. They all left a small offering for Olga.

One morning, when their mothers had gone to wash clothes in the river, Astra and Mara decided to see if the mirror would reveal its secrets on Hugo's behalf. They filled the basin, carried it up, taking care not to slop the water and wet their feet, and put the mirror in place. Mara lit the candles which, by this time, had burned down to small stubs.

"Now!" she announced solemnly.

Into the water Astra dropped a brooch that Hugo had given her for her thirteenth birthday. Lucky thirteen, she had told Mara, who had not been happy when she selected it. They had almost ended up having an argument with Astra saying she had enjoyed her thirteenth birthday, it had been a good day, and Mara saying that she did not think it would work since it was linked to an unlucky number. "For goodness sake, Mara!" Astra had retorted. "Did you feel unlucky for the whole of your thirteenth year?"

The brooch settled at the bottom of the tin basin and Astra, her heart beating fast, lifted her eyes up to the mirror. She saw, reflected, the guttering flame of the two candles and her old familiar face and her hair, which had grown long and was beginning to look ragged, like a gypsy's. She was not as patient as her mother when it came to wielding a brush and they had lost their sharp scissors at one of the camps.

"I can only see myself!" She was bitterly disappointed.

"Let me try," said Mara.

"But you have nothing to put in that Hugo gave you."

"Perhaps it doesn't matter." Mara was slipping off the ring that she wore on the middle finger of her right hand. Astra moved over.

Mara closed her eyes for a second, then, opening them, she let the ring slide into the water. She leaned forward, her lips slightly parted, her breath puffing out to film the mirror. She was concentrating intensely, her eyes dilating slightly. Astra did not dare look at the mirror herself; only the person who had dropped something into the water was allowed to do that.

"I can see him," said Mara. She sat back on her heels, smiling.

"Let me see!" Astra wrenched the mirror around but saw, once more, herself, and the twin candle flames which were dwindling rapidly and turning to black smoke. Mara snuffed them out with her fingers.

"You *didn't* see him, Mara, you *didn't*!" cried Astra. "I don't believe you."

"But I did." Mara picked up the basin. "And I don't care if you believe me or not because I know that I did see him." With her head held high, she took the basin away to pour out the water, leaving Astra squatting alone on the floor, wondering.

Had Mara lied? She had never known Mara to tell lies, except for little unimportant white ones at times, like anybody else. Or had she deluded herself, willing her mind to believe that it was Hugo whom her eyes had seen in the glass? Or did she, perhaps, have the gift that her mother had? Astra could not rule out that possibility. *Was* it a gift? And could it be that she, Astra, had not seen Hugo because she had never really believed in Olga's fortune telling? Without faith, miracles could not happen.

When Mara came back upstairs, she asked, "What did Hugo look like in the mirror?"

"Thin. As if he had been ill. And he was without his glasses. But he was smiling."

When they first came to the farm they went to the local school, but did not have time to settle in properly before it had to close because of lack of heating fuel. Instead, they spent their days roaming about the countryside and helping on the farm, activities much preferred by the two boys. When it was raining, Tomas and Zigi squatted inside the barn door making model airplanes from pieces of scavenged wood. The boys were obsessed by model making and constantly bemoaned the fact that they had no glue or rubber bands or wire—anything that would hold their models securely together. They had to use whatever they could lay their hands on, salvaged nails, odd bits of string, strips of rag. "No string to spare?" they would ask hopefully and their mothers would shake their heads. Every tiny piece of string was cherished and kept carefully rolled up. Every piece of paper was smoothed out and folded and put in a safe place. As for rubber bands! They did not know when they would ever see such things again.

In the evenings Lukas gathered the four young ones together and gave them lessons in history, literature, Latin, and English. They had only one or two books, and the wavering light of the candle made it difficult to read, but they talked a great deal. They could learn languages by listening, Lukas said, and asked them to make a special effort with

English. "I think we may need it. The Americans appear to be coming in our direction. So are the Russians, of course!"

"Are the Germans losing?" asked Tomas in a loud voice, and was immediately hushed by Astra.

"You never know who will hear you!"

No German whom they had spoken to would admit to losing. They were still convinced that Hitler would lead them to victory. There was talk of a new weapon, and had been for months, and some believed that this miracle weapon would reverse their fortunes and wipe the Allies from the map of Europe.

"Herr Mann says the Führer is a great man," said Zigi. "He says we should join the Hitler Jugend."

"You get a uniform and a leather belt and a drum to beat!" Tomas was excited. He had always loved drums. "We saw them in the village today. Lots of the boys belong."

"It would be good fun." Zigi turned to his father. "Please, Father, can I join?"

"No, Zigmunds, you cannot!" Paulis did not often call his son by his full name.

Tomas looked questioningly at his father.

"I doubt if you would be allowed to join—we're not German citizens. And if you were, I wouldn't want you to. I don't mind you playing a drum to make music but I don't want you to march in a uniform beating one." Lukas was choosing his words carefully,. Astra knew, for it would be dangerous to speak openly against the Führer. "And there is no need for you to discuss this any further with Farmer Mann, either, boys. Do you understand?"

News of the war trickled through to them. Anyone who passed by was pressed for news and they went daily to the village to glean whatever information they could. The Russians appeared to be advancing steadily westward, through

Poland, Czechoslovakia, and Hungary. The British, Americans, and Canadians were pushing eastward. In the middle of January the Russians occupied the Polish capital of Warsaw and by the end of the month had crossed the German frontier. They were now on German soil! Herr Mann tramped around the farm with a grim face.

On the eighteenth of February, Budapest, capital of Hungary, fell to the Soviets. On the twenty-eighth, and again the next day, the first of March, Leipzig was heavily bombed by the Americans. Later in the month, they heard that the Russians were driving toward the ports of Danzig and Gdynia in an attempt to cut off Germany's access to the Baltic. Fighting was reported to be fierce. German refugees escaping from both east and west fled into the middle of the country. Some arrived in the village near their farm.

The days were lengthening, the air had turned mild, spring flowers brightened the meadows. Astra and Mara picked flowers and grasses and put them in tins. They swept the floor of the loft every morning and rolled up the blankets and quilts. They took pride in their home. "It's like a nest," said Mara. Astra nodded. It was like an oasis of peace in the middle of the battles that were raging in a fiery ring around them. Could they expect to stay safe inside it?

On the twenty-sixth of March, Gdynia fell to the Russians.

"What if Hugo is still there?" asked Astra, alarmed.

Her father thought it unlikely. "At least, let us hope that he is not."

During the first two weeks of April, Allied air raids were stepped up over Leipzig and Gera. They sat at the door of the loft watching. The sky would light up as if on fire itself. American bombers passed overhead in droves. Searchlights fanned the sky, trapping planes in their beams, but the anti-aircraft fire from the ground was sporadic and seemed to find few targets. Only the occasional plane with an iron cross was to be seen. The Germans were said to be running out of fuel for their aircraft as well.

And then they heard that the American forces were only eighteen miles to the west of Leipzig, less to the south; and the Russians thirty to the east. Which would reach them first?

"It *must* be the Americans!" said Astra.

"Let's keep our fingers crossed," said Lukas.

The local radio station maintained that the German lines were holding, that the Americans were being pushed back. Herr Mann believed it; he knew that no one would ever occupy the Fatherland again. The end of World War I had been the last time that they would ever have to bend their knee to a conqueror. He went on reavowing his belief even when the frequency and number of American planes passing overhead continued to increase. They came both by day and by night, blanketing the sky. The children stood below, gazing up in astonishment.

"I didn't know so many planes existed in the world," said Tomas, craning his head so far back that he almost locked his neck into position.

Food had become scarcer and scarcer. The farm's potato supply ran out. At nights they went to bed hungry. Granny Jansons moaned about cramps in her stomach and Klara cried, not understanding that there was nothing left to eat.

"The Americans will bring food, I expect," said Olga, as she ladled out plates of thin watery soup made from bits of frosted turnip and nettles. "They have lots of food, so it is said. Tins of meat and peaches and butter made from peanuts."

"Chewing gum!" said Tomas. "I hope they bring chewing

gum. And glue and rubber bands. And gigantic balls of string."

"Bananas!" cried Zigi, waving his arms about. "Big, big bunches of fat bananas!"

"Yum yum." Tomas pretended to peel and eat a banana. "What am I, Zigi?"

"A gorilla!"

"Boys!" reproved Kristina. "Careful, now, or you'll spill your soup."

"I don't want it," said Zigi. "It makes me feel sick."

"Eat it!" commanded his father. "There will be nothing else tonight."

In spite of the proximity of battle, Tomas and Zigi continued to roam the fields, chewing strands of grass when their stomachs ached with hunger. They took their fishing tackle and fished along the riverbank. Some days they returned triumphant, carrying a little fish or two, which their mothers grilled on the stove and divided up so that everyone could have a taste, although often that taste seemed to make them more conscious of their hunger. Their clothes hung slackly on them now.

One afternoon, when the boys were fishing, they worked their way farther up river than usual to where a road bridge spanned it. Zigi had just pulled out a small perch and was yelling with excitement when Tomas saw movement up ahead.

"Shush, Zig! Soldiers!"

The soldiers in their gray-green German uniforms were working with something near the bridge. Several had gone underneath.

"Explosives!" said Tomas. "They're going to blow up the bridge."

"What for?" asked Zigi, his eyes opening wide.

They crawled a little nearer on their stomachs, to watch through the long grass.

"To stop the Americans getting through," whispered Tomas. "They can't be far away, Father says."

At that moment, they heard the whine of aircraft overhead and saw, coming in low, half a dozen U.S. fighter planes.

"Run!" cried Tomas.

They hardly had time to drop their lines and the hooked fish and take to their heels before the world erupted around them. This is what hell must be like, thought Tomas, as he ran, panting, faster than he'd ever run in his life. They were running for their lives. They went streaking up the riverbank, across the field, feeling that their lungs would burst. The *rat-tat-tat* of machine-gun fire was loud enough to split their eardrums. Bullets were flying in all directions. They heard the whistle of a bomb and in the next instant saw it explode in the middle of a flowering apple tree in the Manns' orchard. The tree was cleft in two; in the ground was a huge crater.

They reached the farm gate and collapsed against it. They had stitches in their sides. Their faces were brick-red. They couldn't run anymore. They couldn't get their breath. Bullets were bouncing off the cobblestones in the yard.

"This way!" someone was yelling at them. It was Tomas's father, from the door of the farmhouse.

They staggered into the house and followed him down the stairs to the cellar where their families and Herr and Frau Mann were huddled. Granny Jansons's eyes were closed and her lips were moving in prayer.

"Thank God!" Kristina put her arms around Tomas and hugged him.

They waited, as the noise raged around them, expecting

that, at any instant, a bomb would blast them into the sky. And that would be the end of us, thought Tomas, in awe—the very end. Zigi and I would never go fishing again. He looked around. Granny Jansons was not the only one who was praying.

And then the noise ebbed away, and silence fell. A strange silence. It was as if the world was holding its breath. Granny Jansons was the first to speak.

"The good Lord has seen fit to spare us," she said.

Zigi and Tomas went out early in the morning. Zigi wanted to see if his fish was still there. But it was not. There was a hole in the riverbank where they had fished.

They looked upstream to the bridge: there was a hole there, too. The supports were still standing, but the middle of the bridge sagged inward to form a vee, dropping away into the water. The kingfishers and wagtails still skimmed the river's surface as though nothing had happened.

The boys walked on toward the village. The road was littered with shrapnel and spent shell cases. Gingerly they rolled one or two over with their toes, though their fathers had warned them not to touch anything. They didn't want to get their hands blown off, did they? No, nor their feet, either. Especially after yesterday's lucky escape.

At the crossroads stood a line of tanks. Tomas and Zigi stopped and stared at them. The hatch of the leading tank shot up, and out came a black face. The man began to scrub his dazzling white teeth with a toothbrush. The boys gazed in wonder. They had never seen a man with a black face before. Then the soldier spat over the side of the tank, wiped his lips with the back of his hand, his head went down, and the hatch snapped shut again.

"It looks like the Americans have arrived," said Tomas.

8

DURING the weeks that Hugo was fighting to recover his health he thought constantly about his family. Would they have reached Leipzig? Would they have turned back to look for him? Most likely they had made their way to Leipzig, he decided. He wrote to them in January and again twice in February, care of Professor Zimmermann, but so far had received no reply.

It was more than possible, of course, that the letters had not reached them, or that his family had not arrived there, either. Though he had a feeling that they had, for one night he had had a vivid dream in which he had seen Astra in a sequence of kaleidoscopic images: walking along a street, standing in front of a church, pushing open the door of the church. He had recognized the building. It was St. Thomas of Leipzig! Professor Zimmermann had sent him a postcard of it once and he had pinned it to his bedroom wall.

When he had wakened he had jumped up and pulled on his clothes, wanting to set out at once for Leipzig—and would have done so had the Schneiders not cautioned him. He couldn't see properly, his headaches were still bad, there was the incessant danger of air raids, the roads and railways were in a state of turmoil, and he had no pass to travel with.

The scar on his forehead was beginning to heal after long weeks of suppurating, but he remained prone to headaches. They were partly due to his eyes; he was constantly peering and straining to try to make things out and he could not read, which was a great loss. He had to depend on Bettina. She was reading *The Magic Mountain* by Thomas Mann out loud to him—a thick, complex novel about people in a tuberculosis sanitorium in the mountains, lent, among others, by Doctor Braun. Hugo enjoyed hearing Bettina read; her soft, rather slow voice, stumbling sometimes over the longer words, was soothing.

The Schneiders kept very much to themselves. Few people crossed their threshold, except for Bettina's friend, Hilde, and Frau Schneider's widowed sister, who came occasionally on Sundays. They were the only regular visitors. Life had been different at the Petersons' country home in Latvia: there the door had stood open and neighbors had freely come in and out.

"At times like this," Herr Schneider said to Hugo, "and with *them* in power"—he would never use the word Nazis—"it is safer to talk to as few people as possible. It is terrible the suspicion and mistrust *they* have set up—people are afraid of neighbors, and even of friends."

At breakfast one morning, Herr Schneider announced, "It is my day off today and I am taking you to Hamburg, Hugo, to see an eye doctor. Doctor Braun has given me a letter for him."

"That's marvelous, Father!" said Bettina.

"But glasses cost money," Hugo objected.

"I have been saving a little each week," said Herr Schneider. "And the eye doctor is a friend of Doctor Braun's so he has asked him to make the charge as moderate as possible."

"But I can't let you spend any more money on me." Hugo felt troubled. The Schneiders had already been so kind to him that he didn't know how he would ever repay them. When the war was over and he was reunited with his family he would get his father to make them a large present. Or perhaps they could come and visit the Petersons in Latvia.

"We are happy to pay for your eyeglasses, Hugo," said Frau Schneider.

Hugo looked around the table. They were smiling at him, Herr and Frau Schneider and Bettina.

"Thank you," he said.

They set off after breakfast. Herr Schneider had organized a lift into Hamburg on a milk truck. It was Hugo's first visit to the city.

"It was once a fine city," said Herr Schneider sadly. "It has suffered fierce bombing raids, particularly over a few days in July 'forty-three when the bombing was not aimed at military installations or the harbor, but was indiscriminate. We watched from the village. You'd have thought the whole of Hamburg was burning. And the next day a great cloud of black smoke enveloped the city."

They were quiet as the truck drove in through the streets, taking detours to avoid those that were impassable. Many were blocked by piles of rubble. Whole rows of houses stood roofless, gaping open to the sky. They passed people digging in the ruins with their bare hands. They passed people sitting on the pavement with their heads on their knees in utter dejection. A pall of gray dust hung over everything. There had been a raid the night before and fires blazed close to the docks.

The driver dropped them off outside an apartment building that looked as if it had had its front chopped off. It stood open to wind and air like a giant bookcase.

"Look!" Hugo pointed upward. "There are people still living up there!"

A family was sitting in a three-sided room on the second floor. The front wall was missing. They sat there as if on a stage set, in full view of the world.

"How do they get up to it?" asked Hugo. "The stairs are gone."

"By rope."

"But the place might collapse at any time."

Herr Schneider shrugged. "They take their chance. Many people have to."

The next street was a complete wasteland. It was like being on the moon. Nothing had been left standing. The road itself had disappeared. Herr Schneider and Hugo climbed over enormous chunks of fallen masonry, chimney pots, twisted, blackened window frames and door frames, buckled bedsteads, other unrecognizable pieces of charred furniture, a bath full of black scummy water, the chassis of a baby's carriage flattened right down to its wheel base.

They stopped, hearing a child's cry. It seemed to have come from within the ruins.

"It was over here, I think," said Herr Schneider, leading the way through a narrow passage between the rubble. They came into what appeared to be a cave. And that was just what it was, Hugo realized, as his eyes began to adjust to the dim interior—a cave in which homeless people were living. Small amounts of light and air were filtering through apertures in the debris. A lamp with an uncovered flame flickered on a makeshift table. Two people sat slumped beside it. They raised their heads when Hugo and Herr Schneider entered but did not speak. On the floor two small children played with a pile of rubbish. A third, older one, who looked fevered, lay on a filthy mattress. This might have been the one who had cried out.

"Can't we do anything for them?" Hugo asked. But what could they do? They had no money, no food to spare, no medicine. They turned away, and as they came out into the light, a dark shape ran in front of them and scurried into the ruins.

"They tell me Hamburg is swarming with rats," said Herr Schneider.

They walked into the center of town where the eye doctor conducted his business. Until they saw the building that housed his office, Herr Schneider had not counted on finding it still in existence.

The doctor tested Hugo's eyes.

"No wonder you've been having headaches! Your eyeglasses will be ready in one week. Unless I'm bombed out first."

Or the British arrive, thought Hugo, who had been tuning in to foreign stations on Herr Schneider's old radio and had heard that the British and Canadians were making a strong push for the north coast.

Before leaving Hamburg, Herr Schneider took Hugo to see about getting new identification papers and a ration book. They had to wait in line for most of the rest of the day and when they reached the window, the clerk seemed tired and disinterested. All right, she said, after Herr Schneider had talked to her persuasively, fill in the forms and she'd see what she could do about fixing Hugo up with a temporary identity card. "Return in one week."

After they had retraced their steps back through the dark, chaotic streets, they were glad to smell the sweeter, cleaner air of the open fields. They got a lift in a cart for two or three miles but had to walk the rest of the way. They walked in silence, mostly. Each had his own thoughts. Hugo's ran on to his family. I hope the British arrive soon and finish off the war, he was thinking, though not too soon, not before my glasses are ready; but when they do come I will be able to go and find Mother and Father and Astra and Tomas and we will return to Latvia, all together! His longing to see them was so great that it was like a physical pain turning in his stomach.

He talked often about them to Bettina, who wanted to know what Astra was like, what colors she wore, and did she like to read, too? Yes, she liked to read, said Hugo, but she spent more time with people than he did, though even as he was saying so he was aware that nowadays he was seldom on his own, except when he went walking, through the woods, or along the canal banks. He enjoyed following the canals; he liked the way they cut long, straight swathes through the green countryside, and the gentle flow of the water was quieting. What about Tomas? Bettina asked. Did he resemble Hugo? No, he was different, said Hugo, more physical; he had lots of energy, liked to be on the move, fish, make things, get into trouble!

"He is young, of course, only eight going on nine."

"You were the quiet one?"

"I suppose that is true." Bettina was the first person he had ever confided in, apart from Astra. Bettina was easy to talk to; she listened, as though she were really interested, and nodded, interrupting only now and then to slip in another question, to prompt him along. "I talk too much about myself!" he protested.

"No, you don't! I want to hear. You can see my life—it is all here, I have always lived in this cottage. You know my mother and my father. But I do not know your country or your family."

Hugo worried because his family did not know where he was, or even whether he was alive or dead. He knew they must be suffering greatly on his account.

"Very many people are suffering in this war," said Bettina. "Hilde's family has just heard that her brother Karl has been killed on the Hungarian front." She touched Hugo's hand. "Not that it makes it any easier for you, I know that."

Sometimes, wakening on mornings when it was still dark and only a faint glow from the stove illuminated the room, he would get out of bed, disoriented, and stumble halfway to the door. And then he would remember that he was no longer in his room in their old country house in Latvia but in a signalman's cottage in northern Germany. When he could not sleep, he lay in the box bed listening to the rumble of the passing trains and wondered if his family might not be on one of them. They were still packed with refugees. Since the fall of East Prussia at the end of January and the advance of the Soviets through Hungary and Czechoslovakia, many more had joined the bands of displaced people. Herr Schneider saw their faces at the train windows as they flicked past his signalman's box.

A week later, Hugo and Herr Schneider returned to Hamburg to collect the glasses. They were round, unframed, and held together by wire.

"The best I can do, I'm afraid," said the doctor.

"They're beautiful!" said Hugo.

They lay on the doctor's table, glinting in a ray of sunshine. Hugo's hands trembled when he picked them up. He put them on and the world came back into focus after months of seeming to exist behind a swirling mist. He could have wept. He blinked and turned to look at the two men. He saw their smiles, the way the skin crinkled at the corners of their eyes, and the twinkle in the blue eyes of Herr Schneider, and he saw each link in the gold watch chain on the doctor's waistcoat. Hugo went to Herr Schneider and, putting his arms around his shoulders, hugged him, mumbling words of thanks that seemed quite inadequate. Herr Schneider clapped him on the back and laughed with pleasure.

With glasses, an identity card (albeit a temporary one), and a ration book—the basic essentials for survival—Hugo felt equipped to venture out into the world. He had hoped to go to school, but the local high school was seldom open because of air raids and lack of heating fuel. It was too cold yet to sit in unheated classrooms. Most days Hugo walked to the school with Bettina, in case the doors might be open.

"What will it be like, do you think," asked Bettina, "after the British come in? If they come. But it seems that they will. I feel a bit afraid, Hugo."

"I don't think they'll be like the Russians. Or the Nazis." As he spoke, he glanced over his shoulder. To look over one's shoulder had become almost an automatic reflex. He knew little about the British except what he had read in novels by writers like Charles Dickens and Sir Walter Scott. But then an English boy reading *The Magic Mountain* would not get a complete picture of Germany and the Germans, only a few clues. "They sound as if they might not be too aggressive. Though I expect soldiers are everywhere."

"I wonder if the British will open the school again?"

"I expect they might."

"That would please you!" She liked to tease him about burying his head in books.

"I don't suppose I'll be going to school here then, Bettina."

"No?"

"I'll be returning to Latvia. Once I've found my family."

"Of course! I keep forgetting, you've become so much a

part of our family. Once we were three, now we are four! My father always wanted a son, though he says he was very happy when I was born. But my mother couldn't have any more children after me. I shall miss you," Bettina added.

She had a way of speaking out directly, of saying what she felt. He was not so good at knowing what to say in return. Her directness often served to clamp his mouth shut. He wished that he could say what he was thinking at this moment—that he would miss her, too. He watched the gray road unfolding in front of their feet. They continued into the village without saying anything more.

They were going to buy bread at Klinger's. The bell jangled above the shop door as they opened it. The shelves were becoming increasingly empty. Herr Klinger was standing behind the counter with his arms folded across his chest, listening to the radio. He reached out and abruptly cut off the sound.

"Lies, all lies! You cannot defeat a man like the Führer easily. He will lead us to victory yet. *Heil Hitler!*" Turning to the portrait on the back wall, he saluted and looked around to see if Hugo and Bettina were being respectful, also.

Bettina busied herself examining an old calendar on the wall, but Hugo returned the man's stare. Their eyes engaged, and Herr Klinger's narrowed, and then the door opened and Doctor Braun's wife came in.

"Have you any potatoes?" she mumbled, without lifting her eyes to meet the storekeeper's.

"Not many," he answered curtly. He put four wrinkled, sprouting ones on the counter.

"That is all?"

"That is all."

"Bread?" She held out two ration books.

He took a loaf from under the shelf and cut four slices She hesitated. "I don't suppose you have eggs?"

"You suppose right."

Frau Braun went out.

"She is always looking for potatoes. Every day she comes and asks. What do two old people like them want with so many potatoes? It makes me wonder. I have been wondering for some time."

"They have to eat even if they are old," said Hugo.

"But so much?" Herr Klinger tapped his chin with his forefinger. "They are strange, those two, the way they will not let anyone go into the house. What are they worried about?"

"He gives me the creeps, that man," Bettina said to Hugo as they returned home through the wood. "He makes me feel as if someone was walking over my grave."

The next day there was a great stir in the village. The Gestapo went to the Brauns' house and took them away and a young man whom they'd found hiding in the attic. All three went without resisting, without saying a word. Frau Schneider had been walking through the village at the time and had seen them go.

"It was dreadful—to see the look of terror on those faces!" She covered her face with her hands.

"He was a Jew, the young man." Herr Schneider shook his head. "Can you imagine—he had been hiding there for some months, so it would appear, and now they find him when the war is almost over! How ironic life can be!"

"He was the son of an old medical friend of Doctor Braun's, from Berlin," said Frau Schneider. "They say he had been on the run all through the war."

I would like to go and kick Herr Klinger's door down and then I would like to kick Herr Klinger down, thought Hugo, and was surprised by the violence of his feelings. When they were young it was always Astra who had been the one to kick; he had been more inclined to crawl off into the orchard and brood.

"But why did the Klingers set the Gestapo on the Brauns?" asked Bettina. "What good does it do them?"

"Puts them in with the Gestapo, I suppose, though it's a bit late for them to benefit much from that now," said her father. "It's something else, too, I think. Some people just seem to wish evil upon others."

"Some people *are* evil," declared Frau Schneider.

"It is difficult to dispute that," agreed Herr Schneider. "I wish we did not have to shop at Klinger's but we have no choice!" He looked at Bettina and Hugo. "You will be careful of course to say nothing when you are in there? Remember that the Gestapo are still around! And the war is not yet over. Even when it is we shall have to watch what we say—for then we shall be occupied people."

Hugo nodded. He knew full well what that meant.

Throughout the month of April, they heard of the collapse, one after the other, of the German armies, who were being driven back on the various fronts by the British, French, Canadian, American, and Russian forces. A night seldom passed for the Schneiders and Hugo without an air raid alert. The siren would go off if Allied planes were anywhere within a wide range. They took refuge in a bunker in the garden. The bombers attacked Hamburg, Bremen, Kiel, Hanover. Their main targets now were airfields, rail centers, oil refineries, oil storage depots, U-boat shelters, military installations. Hanover fell to the British Ninth Army.

Hugo gleaned most of his information from foreign radio stations, though he had to be extremely careful, for listening to an enemy broadcast was a crime punishable by death.

Sometimes, at noon, he managed to pick up the BBC's German language bulletin. It began with the opening chords of Beethoven's Fifth Symphony and the words *"Achtung! Achtung! Hier spricht London!"* Attention, here speaks London! He kept the volume turned down low and Bettina would stand at the window on guard.

"Like a rising tide," said the newscaster, "the British and Canadian armies are spreading over northern Germany and northern Holland."

On the nineteenth of April, Hugo heard that Leipzig had been enveloped by the Americans.

"Leipzig!" he exclaimed and then, as Bettina was about to speak, he put his finger to his mouth and bent his head again.

"General Hodges is attacking from the east and west, and General Patton's forces have come under heavy shell fire from dug-in positions along the perimeter defenses of the city, manned mostly by SS troops."

Hugo hoped that his family would not be anywhere near the perimeter defenses of the city. The SS were the crack divisions of the German army.

"British tanks are seventeen miles from Hamburg," continued the news reader, "and the outskirts of Lüneburg have been reached by the 11th Armored Division who are eight miles from the Elbe.

"Consistent gains are also being made in the direction of Stuttgart and up the eastern bank of the Rhine by the French First Army. . . ."

So the British were only seventeen miles away from Hamburg!

By the twenty-first of April they had cut in two the road linking Bremen and Hamburg. "Germans are fighting to the limit to save their two great ports and naval bases, Bremen and Hamburg. . . ."

And on that day also, Leipzig fell to the American First Army.

Hugo felt dazed. Everything seemed to be happening very fast now; the German forces were going down one after the other, like a pack of cards toppling, and soon the war must end. No one expected a reversal of Germany's fortunes at this late date. The Russians were besieging Berlin, Hitler's stronghold. Even Herr Klinger had ceased to talk about the Führer rallying. Most days the door of his shop remained closed and its blind pulled.

As soon as an armistice was declared, Hugo intended to set out on his journey, and he planned to go even though the roads and railways would be in a state of chaos. He would walk all the way, if necessary. Continuing to listen to the radio, he heard that the Americans and Russians had met up on the Elbe, thus cutting Germany in two. Berlin was reported to be "in its death throes," though the whereabouts of the German leader were not known. It was rumored that he had fled the country, was in South America, or Japan; that he was regrouping his forces; that he had committed suicide.

At the end of the month came the momentous announcement: "Adolf Hitler is dead!"

Hugo felt himself begin to tremble. He ran to the door to shout to Herr Schneider, who was working in the garden. "Hitler is dead!"

Herr Schneider took the news rather more soberly. It was the end of an era, albeit a bad one, at least from his point of view, although many of his fellow countrymen would certainly not agree. Most, in fact, would not. But what would face them now? They could not expect to be well treated by the occupying army of a power with whom they had been engaged in total war. And they could not expect Allied soldiers to differentiate between Germans who were pro-Hitler and those who were not.

"I fear we shall all be tarred with the same brush," said Herr Schneider.

Later it was learned that Hitler had withdrawn to his bunker with his wife, Eva Braun, whom he had married only the day before, and there they had both committed suicide. She had swallowed cyanide, he had shot himself in the mouth. Their bodies had then been taken out into the garden by loyal supporters, gasoline poured on them, and set alight. The Allies were not to be permitted to put their hands on the body of their beloved Führer!

On the third of May, General Wolz, commander of the garrison in Hamburg, surrendered the city to General Montgomery, commander of the British Second Army, to save it from further bombardment.

Hugo and Bettina watched the British tanks and armored cars pass through the village. It was observed that Herr Klinger had removed the picture of the Führer from his back wall and the placard saying *For the glory of the Fatherland* from the front window.

On the seventh of May, 1945, the German army surrendered, unconditionally. The war in Europe was over.

Herr Schneider knew that Hugo was anxious to find his family but cautioned him to wait a little while, until things settled down a bit. "How can you possibly walk all that way? It must be about two hundred and fifty miles."

"He must go, Father," said Bettina. She spoke sadly.

"I'm sorry," said Hugo.

"You don't have to be sorry," said Frau Schneider. "We understand very well. We would expect Bettina to do the same for us."

She gave him a blanket, his ration book, and some food—a few cold potatoes, a couple of slices of bread, and a hard-boiled egg, all that she could spare. More than she could spare, he knew. Herr Schneider gave him a few marks.

"I'm not sure if the money will be any good, it's not worth much, anyway, but take it, go on—take it!"

Hugo thanked them.

"At least the weather is warmer now," said Bettina, who was trying to talk brightly.

They walked with him to the end of the road.

"And remember, lad," said Herr Schneider "that you can come back when you want to. You will always have a home here."

Hugo embraced each of them in turn, Bettina last, and when he stepped back from her he saw there were tears in her eyes. She had told him she would probably cry, she hated saying good-bye to people. His own eyes were not totally dry. How he hated leaving these good people! But how he wanted to find his own kin! Raising his arm in farewell, he turned and walked off without looking back. His progress along the military-dominated roads was slow and difficult, reminding him of their journey through Latvia to the coast. But there was one big difference—there were no air raids. And that meant he could sleep peacefully at nights in a meadow, or a wood, wrapped in the blanket given to him by Frau Schneider. The grasses were knee-deep in the meadows and the trees were bedecked with blossoms: apple, pear, cherry, linden. The towns were a different matter: places of misery, ruined and squalid, they were proving to be breeding grounds for typhoid and dysentry, with their fractured water and sewage pipes leaking through the rubble. He avoided them where possible.

As he went farther south the days—and nights—became warmer. On occasion, he crept into a barn and slept among the cows. Farmers' wives would give him milk to drink and usually a crust of bread. Once or twice he arrived in a place when the Americans were giving out food to refugees and by joining the line he received a tin of spongy pink meat they called Spam and a bar of chocolate.

He walked most of the way, but sometimes managed to hitch a lift for a mile or two in a tradesman's van or on a farmer's tractor. He was stopped regularly at checkpoints, but after he told his story was allowed to proceed. Bands of refugees clogged the roads, most of whom did not know where they were going. Some said they were trying to head homeward; others that nothing would persuade them to do so, not if the Soviets were in control of their country. The Allies had not realized that they would have such hordes of displaced people to cope with, so when someone came along like Hugo who could declare a known destination, they waved him on.

He arrived on the outskirts of Leipzig at the end of May, to find yet more scenes of devastation. As in Hamburg, whole streets had disappeared, and vegetation was growing out of the rubble. Weeds took little time to establish themselves. A green bush stuck incongruously out of a bomb crater. Rose bay willow herb was running riot. There was a terrible stench in the air—of charred remains and putrefying bodies. Two men passed him carrying a woman on a lashed-up stretcher. Her head lolled over the side, her face was a grayish-purple. He saw other people with makeshift stretchers. There appeared to be no ambulances. German soldiers were hobbling about in tattered uniforms and boots held by string. Hugo watched as a man, stalking an unsuspecting squirrel, pounced, grabbing it between his hands. Then he banged its head against a stone. Hugo winced. It would be for the pot, no doubt. Everywhere people were scavenging for food, scratching around with torn, bleeding hands. He could scarcely bear to look at them. In front of him, a skinny horse pulling a cart suddenly collapsed. The driver got off to try to raise it up, but its head had rolled over and it was frothing at the mouth.

"Hunger," said the driver, who looked half starved himself.

Hugo walked on in a daze, trying to find his way to the suburb where Otto Zimmermann lived. Most people whom he asked for directions could not help. They frowned at him, perplexed. Often he had to repeat his question. They would shrug. They had not heard of the street, no longer knew where anything was. Their faces were etched with dust, their eyes abstracted. He saw one man digging frenziedly in a ruined house and a woman pulling at his clothing and crying, "It's no use, Wolfgang, they must be dead, it's too long ago." The man went on digging, throwing earth and rocks over his shoulder.

Hugo stopped in front of one house that had been sliced in two, like the apartment building he had seen in Hamburg, with the remaining half left standing exposed to the air. He gazed at the patterned paper on its walls and the bathroom fixtures still standing in position. The floors sloped downward and the few remaining sticks of furniture looked as if they might come tumbling out at any second. What had become of the people who lived there? While he stood, the walls began to tremble and shift before his eyes. He watched the house slide down, miraculously with hardly a sound, and become yet another pile of debris. Dust rose from it like smoke. He moved on.

Along streets that had been cleared, American army vehicles sped. American soldiers stood on guard outside public buildings. The Stars and Stripes fluttered from masts where until recently the swastika had flown.

It took Hugo most of the day to track down the Zimmermanns' street. A pearly-gray dusk was creeping in around the trees and rooftops as he turned into it. His throat was parched, as if lined by the city's dust. On his journey he had not allowed himself to think more than a step ahead or anticipate the reunion with his family, but now that he had come so far, excitement quickened in him.

Most of the houses in this street were large, set in good-sized gardens. He was looking for number ten. Lights shone from number two; four was dark and all its windows had been blown out; six had been bombed and was caved in in the middle. He hurried on, his heart thumping. Number eight was damaged, had a chimney missing and most of its windowpanes, but it still stood. A high wall and tall trees separated it from its neighbor. Two of the trees were lying across the wall, which was ruptured at these points. They looked as if they had been felled by lightning. Or a bomb. Hugo broke into a run, then halted, abruptly.

Number ten was a heap of rubble: it must have sustained a direct hit.

9

AFTER THE WAR everything connected with ordinary every-day life in Germany came to a standstill: factories and offices closed, food ran out, shops put up their shutters, trains languished in sidings. There was much looting. Disorder was the order of the day.

"It is always so at times like these," said Lukas, as they watched a steady procession of men, women, and children with hand carts passing in the road. The carts were of all shapes and sizes: some with a single wheel, like a wheelbarrow; some with two wheels, others, four. They walked in an orderly way, as Germans were wont to do, observed Kristina; the fortunes and misfortunes of war did not seem to have disturbed that trait. People pushing empty carts kept to one side of the road and those returning with them laden, to the other. A china factory three miles up the road had been broken into.

"But they're stealing dishes!" said Astra.

"There are no rules for anyone to follow anymore. And, Astra, if that factory was full of food we would be out there, too, with our cart."

Astra blushed. Her father had spoken gently but it had been a rebuke. She had not meant to sound prudish or judgmental. She knew that people were desperate, had been deprived of so much for so long, from food and fuel and proper clothing right down to the trivial things like the rubber bands and glue that the boys were always raving on about. But it was food that occupied most of their thoughts, even the boys, and they spent much of their energy in its pursuit. They were on the verge of starving. Granny Jansons' arms and legs stuck out from her clothing like twigs. They were all bone-thin and their energy was at a low ebb. Some people were reputed to be eating raven and crow and even dogs.

"If we have to stay here much longer we might come to that ourselves," said Lukas. Every chicken in the farmyard had been taken and slaughtered by German soldiers during the closing stages of the war. Every reasonably edible potato had been commandeered also, and the new crop was not yet ready. Most of the cows had gone for meat a long time ago, with only one left for milking.

They were in limbo again, waiting for the next stage in their lives to begin. They hoped that the Americans were going to help them to go home, back to Latvia. They talked about it, saying, when we get home, we shall do this and that, although Lukas would purse his lips and warn them not to count on anything. If the Russians were to stay in the Baltic states then they would not go back. In any case, their first move would be to a camp where refugees were being collected up to be repatriated.

The older members of the families were preoccupied with thoughts of their impending removal; Tomas and Zigi less so. They got on with their lives, were seldom indoors. One of their ploys was to go into Gera and follow the Americans about. These soldiers in their funny squashed hats intrigued them, the way they chewed gum and smoked cigars. They moved so languidly compared to the German and Russian soldiers, who had walked as if they were stiff-legged and stiff-armed. Not now, of course. Any German military that they saw were prisoners, and they shambled and dragged their feet.

Tomas and Zigi, on the heels of the Americans, would wait until they tossed away their cigarette and cigar butts and then swoop down on them, arms and legs flying, in competition with a number of other small boys. They stuffed them into their pockets to bring back for their fathers, who picked out the tobacco and smoked it in their pipes. Sometimes the soldiers would give them chewing gum or, occasionally, a bar of chocolate.

"They must have millions of chewing gum factories in America," said Tomas.

"I want to go to America," said Zigi.

"You are going back to Latvia, Zigi, you know that!" said Mara.

"If I can't go to Latvia, I mean." He shifted a wad of well-chewed gum to the other side of his mouth. He and Tomas were agreed: you didn't feel so hungry when you chewed gum, even after it had lost all its taste.

"If you swallow that stuff, you will stick your insides together!" said his grandmother, sitting up. It was seldom that she roused herself nowadays. Most of the time she lolled in a corner, mumbling to herself. She smiled only when young Klara, who had found her feet, came tottering toward her. She had made Klara a doll from plaited straw. The doll's name was Anna.

"Want dress for Anna," said Klara.

"No dress," said Granny Jansons, shaking her head. "We have no cloth. We have no scissors. We have no thread. We are all in rags. Like scarecrows!"

Mara found a piece of sacking and tied it around the straw doll's body.

When her mother was unwell Mara looked after Klara. In the last few months Olga's health had not been good. None of them were very fit, could not expect to be, but Olga had a tendency to be anemic and it was obvious from her pallor that her blood count was low. She needed iron, but there was no meat to be had. And she coughed at night, a harsh, insistent cough that racked her body.

There were times when Astra, in spite of being low in energy, would feel restless and go off on her own for a walk. She hated being cooped up with so many people. Nights were especially difficult with Granny Jansons muttering and snoring and Klara fretting and various other members of the families coughing and wheezing. And every now and then someone would call out in his sleep in the middle of a nightmare.

She had her own nightmares. In them she saw Hugo running at the end of a desolated, smoking street, running and running, with his arms stretched out and she would think he was screaming although she could not hear him. She would awaken in a cold sweat and her heart would be hammering as if it were she herself who had been running and screaming. After that, it would be difficult to go back to sleep. She knew her mother was often awake at night, too; she sensed it. Her mother lay quietly, not tossing and turning. She seldom allowed anyone to see her anxiety.

Mara did not mind the communal living so much; her nature inclined her to be cheerful and not to brood, and she enjoyed playing with Klara and making the loft neat and tidy. She was patient, even with her grandmother. Astra wished she could be more like Mara. She knew that she should not resent having to live night and day with nine other people, and, indeed, would not think of complaining about it for she was well aware that they were lucky to be alive. They had survived the war! That was the most important thing, as her father had said to her only the day before, and now they must look to building a new future, wherever that might be. She had not liked the way he had said wherever that might be: it suggested that he did not believe they would return home.

"And now that the war is over we shall be able to make a real effort to find Hugo," he had added. "As soon as some kind of order is restored and communications are working again, we shall begin."

That thought cheered Astra as she walked today, keeping to the roads as her father had commanded her to do. "It would be a mistake to think that everywhere is safe just because the war is over. There are many stray, desperate people wandering about." Men, he meant; men who might attack her. She heeded his words. They had lived with danger continuously for the last six years. It was only the forms of it that had changed. Their senses were sharpened to scent trouble from a long way off.

Just outside the village, she saw, up ahead, two American soldiers changing a tire on their armored car. She slowed and wondered whether to turn. But you could not be suspicious of everyone, and they looked all right. They were quite young, certainly no more than twenty years old, and a long way from home. As she was. They lifted their heads to greet her.

"Hi! Do you speak English?"

"A little."

"You German?"

She shook her head. "Latvian."

They were not sure where Latvia was. She drew a map in the road, in the dust with a piece of stick.

"The Baltic," she said. "North." She pointed.

Ah, they said, the Russians were in there.

"To stay?"

They shrugged their shoulders. Who knows? Nobod knew anything; at least, they didn't. But they'd heard tha Germany was going to be divided up between the four Allied powers—America, Britain, France and Russia—and they thought they themselves would be pulling back west soon to let the Russians come in.

"You mean the Russians will be coming *here*?"

"Well, that's what the rumors say."

Astra ran home, alarmed, to tell the news to her father. He did not look surprised.

"If they do we shall just have to move west ourselves and try to keep in the American zone."

But how? she wanted to know. They had no money left, their savings had long since gone, and the mark was more or less worthless anyway. Also, their rations had run out, as had their energy. And the trains were not running.

Tomas and Zigi had found a train, in a siding. They had been coming back from fishing when they'd heard a hubbub of voices and, following the sound, tracked them to the railway line. Dozens of people were swarming around the train. It was a goods train.

"Come on, Zig!" cried Tomas. "There might be food."

Men passed them carrying boxes, women were struggling with pieces of leather in their arms. People were crawling over the wagons like ants. The boys had trouble getting near. They found one that nobody was interested in and clambered up to look inside. Tomas, who had gone first, could scarcely believe what he saw.

"Zigi, you'll never guess!"

"Chewing gum."

"No. Even better—Uhu!"

" Zigi, his hands clutching the rim of the ed inside. He looked down into a pool of king, clear-colored liquid. It had the familiar, smell of acetone. He dipped a finger in. It came ut sticky. "It *is* Uhu," he said in awe.

e Uhu containers had been pierced and that was why glue was loose inside the wagon. Imagine—a whole uck full of Uhu! And nobody wanted it but them. But how were they to get it home?

"Come on, Zig!" shouted Tomas.

They raced the couple of miles to the farm and rounded up all the old tins and bottles they could find, then back they went to the train to scoop up the precious glue.

"Think of all the airplanes we'll be able to make, Tom!" cried Zigi.

By the time they had finished they had almost as much glue on their hands, faces, and clothes as they had in the tins and bottles. But they did not mind. They were happy! They could not remember being so happy for a long time.

As they were about to turn for home they saw that people were still pulling huge cow hides out of another wagon. The pieces of leather were about a yard and a half square.

"Let's try and get one," said Tomas.

Some hides had been yanked out and tossed on the embankment, abandoned in favor of better ones. The boys seized one each.

"They weigh a ton," groaned Zigi.

They could not possibly carry the hides—they were bigger than the boys were—so they dragged them with one hand while clutching the Uhu containers in their other hand and under their arms. By the time they reached the barn they were exhausted.

"What have you been doing?" cried Tomas's mother. "Is that glue you've got? We'll never get it off your clothes!"

But she was pleased to see the leather. All their shoes had huge holes in the soles. The next day, the two fathers cut new soles for everyone's shoes and stitched them on with twine donated by Farmer Mann. In return, they soled his boots. They also traded some pieces of leather with a woman in the village for trousers for the boys. They took the remaining leather with them when they were removed to a refugee transit camp run by the Americans and used it as barter for food and clothing. Cut up into small pieces, it was to last a long time.

They were in the camp for John's Day, a very special day for Latvians, when they celebrate the summer solstice. On its eve, the twenty-third of June, all the Latvians in the camp gathered to light bonfires, built from old ammunition boxes, and sing special John's Day songs. Many of the other refugees—Poles, Greeks, Hungarians, Yugoslavs, Estonians, Lithuanians—followed suit and lit fires of their own and sang their own songs. Sparks of fire flew up into the night sky. The singing seemed to fill the earth; no other sound could be heard. The crowd swelled to a vast throng. There were fourteen thousand refugees in the camp. They were smiling as they sang, and hopeful.

Astra sang with the rest, yet her heart was sad. Hugo was not in the compound. As soon as they had arrived she and Mara had done a thorough search.

The camp, an old German army barrack, consisted of long huts, each one housing several refugee families. It was midsummer and stiflingly hot. Doors were left wide open in daytime, and whatever windows could be pried loose. And the gates of the camp were not locked—they could walk out into the surrounding countryside any time they chose.

Within the huts they created their own physical spaces by suspending blankets over ropes, and inside these areas the

Petersons and Jansons tried to carry on life more or less as they had before, establishing a structure and rhythm for their days. They tidied their space, swept it clean, spent time talking together as a family. They missed the farm—it had come to seem like home—but they hoped that this would merely be a stopover, the first stage of the journey which would take them back to their real home.

One of their main concerns was still food. The Americans had not yet managed to get supplies organized for refugees. For themselves, yes—that they could see from the state of the refuse bins outside the U.S. army camp.

The refugees' diet consisted for the most part of macaroni, plain macaroni that had been boiled in water, without any pretensions to sauce or flavoring. Each family was given a bucket and one member went and lined up at mealtimes. Then, according to the number in the family, scoops of macaroni were ladled into the bucket. It was gray and slimy and even though they were almost starving they found it difficult to get down. The boys started to gag as soon as they saw the bucket coming.

After a few days, they carried the bucket to the latrines and dumped the macaroni and set about finding other ways of procuring food, outside the camp. They bartered with the few things they had, picked wild mushrooms and berries. And the boys went scavenging at the dump where the rubbish from the Army barrack was brought. Every morning, they went there and rummaged before the Pole who was in charge set it alight. Lifting out rotten oranges from the tops of crates they discovered good ones nestling underneath in pieces of soft white paper. Beautiful, round, gleaming, sweet-smelling oranges all the way from California! They pressed them to their noses and saliva ran in their mouths. Carefully they peeled the skin, going around and around until it hung in one long curling piece that they laid to one side. That would not be wasted, either. It could be put in hot water to make a drink. Then they broke the fruit into segments and put one between their lips. Juice squirted into their mouths and they laughed with joy.

On other occasions they found potatoes that had begun to sprout but were perfectly edible, dented tins of tomatoes, Spam, corned beef, peaches, apricots, pears, sweetened milk. They also found half-full packets of cigarettes, boxes of matches, chewing gum still in its wrapping, a fountain pen, automatic pencil full of lead, half-used bars of soap, socks, underpants, microscope lenses, a pair of boots that fitted Paulis, shoelaces, a shirt with two buttons missing for Lukas, colored glossy magazines from America which Astra and Mara pored over for hours in amazement. They gazed at the girls with their shiny red lips, smooth golden skin, gleaming hair, and beautiful clothes. Could they ever look like that? Eyeing each other, they saw hair like straw, ragged fingernails, hands weathered from rough work, outgrown cotton dresses bleached from sun. But perhaps anything was possible in a land where milk and honey was said to flow.

And then news came to the camp about the division of Germany: the Americans were to be in control of the south, the French of the southwest, the British the northwest, and the Russians the east, which would include the area in which they were now living. A buzz of concern ran through the camp. Lukas went to see the American commandant.

"We shall be making provision for all those who don't want to stay in the Soviet zone," he told Lukas. "We'll be shipping you out by train, although I can't say where. As you must know, the whole of this damned country is in a state of chaos! There are millions of people wandering about homeless. We just don't know what to do with you all."

Two days later the camp was evacuated by train. There

were no passenger compartments, only coal tenders open to the sky. The refugees were herded in, thirty or forty to a car. They had no room in which to stretch their legs or lie down. They had to sit on their belongings.

As the commandant had said, no one had any idea of their destination. We're like human flotsam, thought Astra, to be tossed to and fro wherever the tide takes us. Where would they be washed up? Perhaps they would travel the railways of Europe for the rest of their lives. They were heading southwest, they could tell that from the sun. Toward Bavaria, thought Lukas, though from previous experience they knew that it was likely that the train might turn about at any moment and go in a completely different direction.

"When will it ever end?" asked Granny Jansons, clutching her stomach. She had been having bad pains for several days. "When will we get home? I thought the war was over!"

Lukas found a doctor in one of the cars who came and examined her, but he said, of course, that there was nothing he could do. He had no medicine. He could not even prescribe rest. And the jolting would certainly not do her any good.

The day after they set off in the train, the weather turned unseasonal, and the rains came. Soon everyone was soaking wet. One man in their cart had an old black umbrella; he sat huddled under its broken rib cage and bits of tattered cloth reading a book, seldom lifting his eyes from the page. He was reading about Egypt at the time of the pharaohs, Astra saw, by craning her neck. She was not surprised by anything that people did on these journeys. Her father often sat and read Ovid or Cicero, and she would see him smile with pleasure at a particular passage. Her mother had continued to draw in her sketchbook, using up every scrap of space on every page. She was making a record for Hugo, she said. It pleased Astra to see her mother drawing, head bent, totally intent; it helped renew her hope that they would meet up with Hugo again. In the rain, however, her parents sat like everyone else, crouched as far down into their clothes as they could get, holding pieces of sacking over their heads.

There were two other young children in their car apart from Klara, one a small baby with a purplish-blue face who never cried and who worried Astra every time she looked in his direction. His mother sat with him cradled in her arms, her eyes fastened on his face as if willing him to live. She made no sound, either. She seemed to have no husband, no relative at all.

When the train was shunted into a siding—which it was to be repeatedly in the next few days, often for hours at a time—they jumped out to stretch their legs, all but Granny Jansons and the woman with the baby.

"You must get out, Mother," Olga was urging. "You must go to the toilet. You will feel better if you do."

"Toilet? Where is the toilet?" Granny stared out into the drizzle.

The passengers were dispersing into the woods. Olga and Paulis took an arm each and lifted Granny out.

"Come with me, Tom and Zigi," said Lukas. "I have an idea!"

"What kind of idea, Father?"

"Wait and see!"

They followed him back along the track. He had noticed a shack, a small wooden hut, the kind of place where railmen keep tools. The door hung off its hinges, half the tarpapered roof was missing.

"We're going to take it apart," said Lukas.

The boys looked at him, round-eyed.

"We're going to build ourselves a shelter. We have to be resourceful, do we not?"

"Fantastic!" shouted Zigi, and they set to with gusto. The wood was half rotten, did not resist being pulled apart. In triumph, they carried the planks and the remains of the roof and fistfuls of rusty nails back to the train.

"Going into the timber business?" asked Kristina.

"We are going to make a house," said Lukas.

Paulis, who was good at constructing things, took charge. All the men in their group helped and soon they had erected a roof over the car. Tomas and Zigi ran up and down excitedly, passing up pieces of wood.

"It might not keep the rain out completely," said Paulis, "but it will help."

When they stopped in the next siding people from other cars followed suit. It was amazing how much stuff they were able to rake up. The passengers in the tender behind theirs built a very fine roof rising up into a peak so that the water would run down. The men were proud of it. They walked up and down, their hands on their hips, admiring it.

"I am not so sure about that," said Paulis, shaking his head.

The first tunnel that they went through, the roof was demolished. Tomas and Zigi stifled their laughter behind their hands. Even the adults smiled. And the next time they went into a siding the men in the following car rebuilt their roof, making it lower. The range of structures that was growing up on the train was amazing. One looked a bit like a pagoda, another had curtains. Paulis found half a tin of yellow paint on a dump and Kristina decorated the sides of their tender with sunflowers. It was a symbol of new life, she said, and of hope.

Some people had put planks underneath the cars between

the wheels, so that they could stretch out at night, but Paulis said they were mad and would not let the boys try it, which they were keen to do. They had once seen an American cowboy film where a man escaping from the bad guys had made his way up the train hanging on upside down between the wheels. Lukas said that people watching their train pass must think it was very strange looking, indeed. A crazy train.

The baby in the silent woman's arms appeared to turn more blue with every passing hour. Kristina made several attempts to talk to the mother, who seemed to be made of stone. She scarcely moved a muscle. Her staring eyes were unnerving. Kristina rubbed the baby's feet, trying to warm them. They felt cold, like ice, she whispered to Lukas. They did not know what they could do: there were no medical services on the train, nor at the stations, except of the most elementary kind. In another car a child of two was close to death; they heard its moaning when the wheels stopped turning.

And then the baby died. They were not sure when it happened, exactly, but after a while Kristina began to think that all life must have left the tiny body. His mother clung to him fiercely, her wide eyes becoming wild when anyone tried to touch either her or the child. At a station Kristina found two Red Cross workers who came and persuaded her to leave the car. "We must take the baby to the hospital," they said. For a moment the stare left the woman's eyes and a flicker of hope could be seen in them. The rest watched her walking up the platform, her shoulders bowed as they carried their burden. Mara burst into tears.

What would become of such a woman? wondered Astra. Her own eyes were burning dry, but her heart felt ready to burst.

They dozed away the time as they were trundled around the railway tracks of southern Germany. The swaying, rollicking movement of the cars, the lack of adequate food, and the warmth built up by the close-packed bodies induced a lethargy that was difficult to break even when they halted and were able to get out. Lukas insisted always that they did, in order to get their circulation moving.

"Jump up and down!" he told them. "Run!" Astra thought she would fall down if she tried to run; her legs buckled even when she walked.

Jerking out of a doze early one morning—they did not really sleep—she sensed that something was wrong in their car. Something was missing. She lifted her head and peered around at the gray sagging heap of bodies. Tomas was sprawled across her mother's lap. Her father sat with his head angled sideways at forty-five degrees, touching the side of the car.

It was a sound that was missing, she realized. She listened carefully. She could hear the slow rumbling of the wheels—at nights they always seemed to crawl—and the man who read about the Egyptians during the day snoring softly. Now she knew what it was!

For the past few days Granny Jansons had been muttering nonstop in her sleep, on and on, until Astra would have to stuff her fingers in her ears. That was the missing sound. Astra looked past the outline that was Mara to Granny Jansons' place. The old woman had toppled over to the left; her head and shoulders were resting against the arm of the man who read about the Egyptians. Her head and shoulders looked slack, as if they would fall back down if you were to try to prop them up. Instinctively, Astra knew that Granny Jansons was dead.

10

HUGO spent three days in Leipzig before heading northward again. He slept out among the rubble the first night, and in the morning wandered around in a daze, trying to take in the information that his family was almost certainly dead, that they had been killed when Professor Zimmermann's house had been blitzed.

On his wanderings he came across a police station and went in. It was being manned by German police still, under the supervision of the Americans. There were blanks on the wall where pictures of Hitler had been removed. Hugo stood in a line for two hours before reaching the counter. He stated his business. A register of refugees? He must be joking! Or of people killed in the bombings? Who would have been able to compile such a list? Who would know where to start? It had been estimated that there were ten million extra people in the country at the moment. And one half seemed to be looking for the other half. What was more, a high proportion of them seemed to be coming in here to do their looking. The policeman's eyes were bloodshot.

"I can do nothing!"

Hugo nodded. As he was coming out of the door a U.S. army car swept into the curb and stopped almost in front of him. The driver leaped out smartly and ran around to open the passenger door. A gold-braided officer stepped out. He looked like an important person. He might be able to help. With a feeling of desperation, Hugo moved toward him. Immediately, the chauffeur jumped between them holding out his arm to bar Hugo's way.

"Please, sir," Hugo blurted out over the top of the man's arm, "could you help me? I am trying to find out what has happened to my family. . . ." He let his voice trail off. He knew his plea to be hopeless. He had witnessed the state of chaos in the country for himself, had seen the bombed ruins, the trains slewed across railway lines, the long straggling lines of German prisoners-of-war being herded along the main roads by Allied forces, the groups of homeless people huddled inside makeshift tents, squatting among ruins, wandering forlornly about.

There was nothing else to do but return to the street that, initially, he had run away from, unable to bear the sight of the heap of masonry that had once been number ten.

He knocked on the doors of neighboring houses where any sign of life could be seen. The inhabitants of number nine were squatters; they had moved in only a month ago. They were from Silesia. They had fled from the Russians. Stay here if you want to, they said, there are plenty of rooms. He spent his other two nights in Leipzig there.

He tried several houses where no one answered his knock, in spite of the fact that lights could be seen behind closed curtains. People were suspicious of knocks on doors by night or by day. Women watched him from behind heavy net screens.

An elderly man came to the door of number two, having

studied him from a downstairs' window beforehand. By then Hugo had learned that it was better not to stand inside the porch but to place himself where he could be clearly seen.

The man nodded. Yes, he had known the Zimmermanns. He and the professor used to play chess together.

"He died some months ago, you know?"

"Before the house was bombed?"

"Several months before—poor old Otto! He was a fine man. I cannot remember exactly when it was that he went. Last autumn sometime, perhaps." He frowned. "My memory is not so good now."

Who had been living in the house when it was hit? Hugo asked. Did he know?

The old man shrugged. There had been many people in the house, as in all the houses; they had been forced to take in lodgers, both civilians and military personnel. He had refugees from East Prussia with him yet. He was tired of listening to the tramp of their feet, they never seemed to be still. He could do with some peace. They said they had peace now but did it look like it? He had heard that shops were being looted in the town center. He was surprised that there was anything in the shops left to loot. He began to ramble.

"Would there have been families at the Zimmermanns', do you think? Children—two younger boys, two older girls about my age? A baby?" Hugo pressed him to try to remember.

"Oh yes, there were definitely refugee families staying at the Zimmermann's. I remember two boys—they used to play up and down the pavement, chasing each other, noisy, the way boys are—and there was a baby, you could hear it crying as if it had the croup. And I seem to think there was a girl about your age."

"Fair hair?"

"They were all quite Scandinavian-looking. They were from the north somewhere. Their language was definitely not German."

"Latvian?"

"Might have been. I am not acquainted with Latvian." The old man sighed. "And to think that all those poor children are dead now! I saw them taking the bodies away. These are dreadful times we are living through, dreadful! I am sorry for you, lad. To lose your family is a terrible thing."

Hugo walked on up the road to the place where the Zimmermanns' house had once stood. Bracing himself, he began to pick his way slowly over its remains, moving aside chunks of masonry, pieces of charred furniture, burned-out pots and pans. He was seeking clues.

He came upon twisted bedsteads, mounds of soggy material that once might have been bedcovers, or rugs, or clothes; jagged shards of glass; a burst, blackened settee; a heavy desktop that had lost its legs; a dented tin bucket. Everything was distorted and discolored. Ruined. Then he saw a toy engine. Ah! But he did not recognize it. His heart, which had begun to beat rapidly, quietened again. And here was a round object that must once have been a ball. Unrecognizable now, to anyone. He frowned, squatted down and reached out to take hold of something that had caught his eye. It was the ear of a teddy bear. Pushing aside a wedge of stone, he lifted it up. The bottom half of the bear was missing but its head, though scorched, was intact. Except for one eye. It was Bruno, Tomas's teddy bear, he was sure that it was!

Dropping the toy, Hugo went lumbering over the top of the ruins, slipping and sliding, grazing his ankles and shins and his hands when he fell forward onto them. On reaching the trees at the edge of the garden, he stopped. He retched. He did not have enough food in his stomach to be sick.

He sighted the smoke from the Schneiders' chimney from half a mile away; he had been watching for it. He imagined he could smell it, that lovely sharp scent of birch wood burning. He broke into a run. During the last part of his journey, jolting along in the back of an empty bread van, he had had the most terrible premonition, as if something was wrong. A vision of the Schneiders' cottage razed to the ground had jumped before his eyes. Lack of food was making him hallucinate at times. Don't be foolish, he had told himself, the war is over, there is no more bombing. But until he saw the chimney and the smoke and the red-pantiled roof and the shelter belt of trees crouching around it, he had been uneasy.

The door stood ajar. He gave it a gentle push and looked into the room. Bettina was setting the table for supper. She was bent forward at the waist laying out three sets of cutlery in neat formation. Now she straightened up, head cocked to one side to assess her arrangement. She straightened a spoon. Her yellow hair gleamed like a beacon in the dim interior. Sensing that she was being watched, she wheeled about and a knife slipped from her hand to the floor, making a little clatter.

"Hugo!" She came rushing to greet him.

He caught her in his arms and hugged her. Her hair smelled sweet against his cheek, a blend of fresh air and woodsmoke.

"I'm filthy," he said. "I haven't had a bath since I left."

She stepped back from him, keeping hold of his hands. "We will put the water on to boil." She laughed. "You are thin, too, though. We will have to fatten you up, won't we, Mother?"

Frau Schneider was at the stove, tending a pot.

"Welcome back, Hugo," she said quietly. She knew what his return meant and realized that although he would be pleased to see them, he would be carrying a heavy heart.

Herr Schneider came in then with his arms full of birch logs. He let the logs topple onto the hearth so that he could embrace Hugo. They all sat down and Hugo told them what he had found in Leipzig.

"I am very sorry, Hugo," said Frau Schneider. "We know how much your family meant to you. You must think of this as your home now, and of us as your family. I don't suppose you will want to go back to Latvia, will you?"

Hugo shook his head. Then he said, as he had done before he left to make his journey south, that he did not know how to thank them.

"When you feel you don't have to keep on thanking us, then we will know that you truly do feel like one of our family. Isn't that right?"

"Yes, Father," said Bettina with a smile.

After supper, Hugo went for a walk in the woods with Herr Schneider. It was a beautiful evening, very calm, very quiet, disturbed only by an occasional birdcall and the soft tread of their feet on the path. The leaves of the birch trees shimmered like gold coins in the late sunshine.

"Time heals, Hugo. You've heard that before, haven't you? It's true, on the whole, even if a few scars are left, as they are bound to be. The scars from this war will take a long time to heal for a great many people. You are young, though, and you have your whole life ahead of you—I know it might sound harsh to hear me say this—but you will have to put your past behind you and start afresh."

As the summer advanced, the slow healing process began working in Hugo. The warm circle of this German family was like a salve to his wounds. The Schneiders gave him their affection, but when he wanted to be alone they did not question that and allowed him to go. Once he walked all night and when he returned in the morning nothing was said, although he was aware from the glances exchanged between Bettina and her mother that he had caused them anxiety and he determined not to give way to the impulse again.

In August the Brauns came back, looking older and frailer. Their Jewish lodger did not return. None of the Jews that had been taken away returned. Many had died in concentration camps, and those who had survived did not want to live in Germany again. They were being helped to go to other countries, the United States, Canada, Australia, New Zealand, as well as to Palestine. A Jewish state was to be established there.

Hugo heard about it on the British broadcasting station that he listened to on the radio. And he learned, too, about the concentration camps in which the Nazis had incarcerated the Jews, and about the gas chambers. It seemed that millions of Jews had been gassed to death. Some had even been turned into soap. *Soap.* How could human beings do such things to one another? Hugo sat, sick and horrified, in front of the radio, unable to speak when Bettina, alarmed, asked him what was wrong. Photographs of skeletons found at Belsen and Buchenwald and other camps appeared in British and American newspapers and magazines. Hugo brought a magazine back from Hamburg and laid it, open, on the kitchen table. "Look!" he said. He did not mean in any way to call the Schneiders to account for the atrocities; he was displaying the photographs out of a need to share his deep sense of shock and revulsion.

The Schneiders were as shocked and distressed as he was. Such pictures had never been seen before, ever. They gazed in horror at the skeletons of men, women, and children huddled together, piled high. In one photograph a long line of naked women holding their children in their arms waited to go into a gas chamber. Bettina sobbed, her face in her hands.

"We had no idea that such appalling things were going on," said Frau Schneider. "Of course we knew that what was happening to the Jews could not be good, but we did not imagine *this*."

Herr Schneider said that he had heard rumors—most Jews had been shipped by rail, after all—but he had not known what to believe. He supposed that he had wanted not to believe so that he could turn a blind eye. He sighed. "We must all bear some guilt—since we allowed it to happen."

"But what could we have done, Gustav?" asked his wife. "We are poor people, we have no power. What would have happened to us if we had stood up and protested? We'd have been marched away double-quick ourselves, you know that. Like your poor brother."

"That is true, Grete. But many Germans must have known and taken an active part—what about all those who helped to run the camps and supply them? They say that trials will be held. It is not going to be easy to be a German in Europe for many years to come. We shall have to hang our heads for a long time."

Soon after the return of the Brauns to the village, the Klingers packed up one night and left before first light. For Bavaria, it was said, where they had relatives. It was in the American zone. The Hamburg area had remained under the administration of the British.

"You made your journey to Leipzig just in time, Hugo,"

said Herr Schneider. "You could not have gone now that it is in Russian hands."

He had heard that his brother had been released from prison, but his home was in the Russian sector of East Berlin. It seemed unlikely he would be allowed to come to the west.

"So still we cannot meet!" said Herr Schneider.

Doctor Braun no longer practiced, but Hugo had formed the habit of calling at his house, to borrow books and to discuss medical and philosophical matters with him. He still hoped to be a doctor himself one day. He enjoyed the hours he spent in Doctor Braun's study among the stacks of dusty tomes and journals. They never spoke of the war, of what had happened to the Brauns when they'd been taken away, or of the fate of Hugo's family.

"Books and learning are a great comfort, Hugo. Even at difficult times. But you must not neglect to spend time with your contemporaries and do all the things that young people do."

Bettina said that Hugo was always streaked with dust when he came back from the Brauns. "Look at you!" She'd brush down his shirt and turn his hands over, palm upward. She'd shake her head mock-seriously and he'd go out to the tap in the yard and wash.

At the beginning of September, the local school reopened. There was a shortage of teachers—many had died in battle or in air raids—and so some subjects could not be taught. Science classes were in disarray because of the lack of equipment and materials. But the pupils managed, one way or another, the older ones helping the younger, and a few elderly teachers came out of retirement. Doctor Braun was persuaded to teach biology a few hours a week.

There was no Greek teacher so Hugo worked at that

alone, able to do so since he had been well grounded by his father. While studying Greek he found that he could think of his father more calmly; it proved to be a kind of solace for him and brought him closer to the memory of Lukas. He would talk to him in his head, discussing passages from Plato or Aristotle. He understood what his father had meant when he had said that the study of ancient languages gave one a feeling of continuity and timelessness and therefore kept one in touch with the grander scheme of things.

His Latin teacher also taught history. She disliked talking about events following 1914, the beginning of World War I. That was her sticking point. Hugo tried to get her to talk about the Baltic states. They had always been buffer states, she said: that was their misfortune. That he knew to be only too true. And their future, what did she think that would be? he asked. How could she predict the future of any part of Europe, she did not have a crystal ball? She lifted her shoulders in a shrug. There was Germany split in two between east and west! Would it stay that way? Probably. And it looked as if Estonia, Latvia, and Lithuania would remain part of the Soviet bloc. She did not think Russia would be prepared to let them go. Hugo nodded; that was how it appeared to him, too.

He was pleased that school had resumed, for now the days had a rhythm that helped him to cope with the anguish that gnawed away inside him. Surfacing into the morning, he would first experience a devastating sense of loss and grief, which always assailed him on waking—the knowledge of his family's fate seemed to be something that he had to relearn each new day—and then he would smell woodsmoke and porridge cooking and he would hear Frau Schneider moving around and he would think, school today! and throw back the quilt and get up at once to go outside and douse his head with fresh cold water from the tap.

Frau Schneider baked a cake for Hugo's fifteenth birthday, which fell on the twenty-fourth of September, 1945. She made it with dried egg powder and liquid paraffin instead of fat and beat up some parsnips with a little sugar to make a cream filling and topping. On the top she had etched his name into the mixture, and the numbers one and five.

"I'm sorry, Hugo—no candles!" she said as she set it in front of him.

"It looks wonderful!"

The cake was golden and well-risen. Frau Schneider baked excellent bread and cakes and made delicious meals with few ingredients. Everything was scarce. In the cities people were starving. Frau Schneider brewed tea with blackberry and strawberry leaves, used beechnut oil or liquid paraffin for fat, rhubarb juice for vinegar. Her daughter had inherited her flair for cooking and improvising.

Hugo stood to cut the cake. As he looked down on it, knife suspended, he could not help but remember birthday celebrations in Latvia, with special food set out on the table, and all the family gathered around. He saw the food, the table, the faces. He had to lay down the knife and take off his glasses for a moment and pass the back of his hand over his eyes.

The images always seemed to come at moments unbidden—in fact, against his bidding, for he had thought of the danger beforehand and had instructed himself to stay within the present and not to look back. He had done his looking back earlier in the day, had risen at first light and walked alone, remembering how he had walked with Astra one year before on the day that they had left Latvia. One whole year! In some ways it seemed like it was only yesterday, her face was still so fresh in his mind, her voice in his ear clear as she chattered to him; but in others, it was more like a lifetime and then she could seem like an insubstantial being adrift in a swirling mist. Once or twice, he thought, in a panic, I cannot remember her face, or Tomas's either, or Mother's or Father's. He had no pictures of any of them. That was an extra pain to bear. All his possessions, the few he had brought from home, had been in the rucksack lost at the railway station in Gdynia.

He replaced his glasses and picked up the knife again. He should not have let his mind wander. Bettina joked about his absentmindedness, said he was like a professor. He glanced around the table at the Schneiders, who were waiting for him to cut his cake. Their patience seemed inexhaustible. Now if it were Astra, she would be saying, "Come on, Hugo, get a move on, don't take all day!" He must put that thought away, at once! He looked back down at the cake so beautifully risen and golden. His fifteenth birthday cake.

"Are you all right?" asked Bettina softly.

He nodded.

"Even though there are no candles, you can still make a wish," said Frau Schneider.

What wish could he make? With his family dead, what was there left to wish for? But no, he must not think like that. He had to be positive. He was constantly trying to send signals to his brain to tell it so. Eventually, he supposed, if he persisted, it would get the message. When he had confronted the Zimmermanns' bombed house in Leipzig he had wondered if he wanted to go on living, with the rest of his family dead. At times he did not, when he felt tired or overcome by grief; then he wished that he could close his eyes and sleep forever and forget all the things that had happened. You have your whole life ahead of you, Herr Schneider had said. On bad days that thought appalled him. But there were more good than bad days now. You can be a doctor and help many people, Doctor Braun had told him; it is a good and a rewarding life.

"Wish!" said Frau Schneider. "There are many good things left to wish for, Hugo, in spite of everything."

He closed his eyes and wished for the happiness of these three people gathered together to help celebrate his birthday, and then, after a moment's hesitation, for some happiness for himself, also. Until now, he had not felt a right to any; the death of his family had seemed to rule that out. "Well done, twin!" he thought he heard Astra's voice say in his ear. "Don't let the gremlins get you!"

He opened his eyes and plunged the knife into the golden cake and the Schneiders applauded and cried, "Bravo! Happy Birthday, Hugo!"

11

THE PETERSONS and Jansons were in southern Germany for Astra's fifteenth birthday, in the small medieval town of Esslingen on the Neckar River. The town was amazingly unspoiled and peaceful; it had escaped the heavy bombing suffered by most German cities and towns. They had arrived only the day before from a camp in northern Bavaria where they had spent the previous two weeks. They had been moved at short notice, as usual, so there had been no time to think of any kind of birthday celebration.

"I don't want to celebrate my birthday this year," said Astra. "How could I possibly?" With Hugo missing, she meant, but did not need to say. He was much in all their minds. At the last camp they had looked for him and drawn another blank, yet again.

They were now firmly inside the American zone and had been billeted in a four-room apartment.

"A proper house," said Tomas in awe, going from room to room, followed by Zigi close on his heels, pushing him in the back in his eagerness to see, too. "With windows and curtains. And all the windows have glass in them!"

The apartments had formerly been inhabited by German workers and their families and been requisitioned by the Americans for refugees.

"Where have all the Germans gone?" asked Tomas.

"Housed elsewhere, I presume," replied his father, knowing that that would not make them popular with the Germans who had been evicted to provide housing for them.

Tomas and Zigi were given one room to sleep in, Astra, Mara and Klara another, and the parents slept on sleep sofas in the other two rooms, which served as living rooms during the day. There was also a kitchen with a stove and a toilet with a lavatory, not a flush one, but, still, it was a lavatory to be used by the nine of them only. For showers they were to go once weekly to the Flieger Schule—the Pilot's School—now another Latvian refugee camp.

"Is all this just for our two families!" asked Olga. "Are you sure they won't move anyone else in, Kristina?"

"No, we were told only two families to an apartment." Kristina was admiring the view from their fourth floor window. Right in front of their block were municipal gardens, which had been divided into vegetable allotments for the townspeople, and beyond was the river lined with poplars. On the opposite bank stood a narrow strip of houses flanked by trees and behind them stretched a long red wall, the boundary of a huge vineyard. And to the right of that sat the old fortified city. Kristina was thinking how pleasant it would be on balmy summer evenings to stroll along the riverbank.

"It's like a palace, this place," said Mara, holding out her arms. "Like some of the apartments in the American magazines."

"A little, perhaps," conceded Astra. "But not too like." Those apartments had been luxurious, with huge windows from floor to ceiling and carpeting that went from wall to wall and big, deep sofas and armchairs. The furniture in their apartment was worn and shabby and somewhat sparse—in the living rooms, apart from the sleep sofas, there were only four unpainted wooden chairs and a table—but they were delighted with every single stick of furniture. And it looked as if they were going to be allowed to stay for a while without having the threat of being moved on hanging over their heads.

"After a year on the road—and the railways!—it will be good to settle for a bit," said Kristina. "And perhaps the Russians will withdraw from our country at some point and then we shall be able to go back."

Most of the refugees continued to nurse that thought. It was not impossible, they reasoned, that the Allies would intervene and demand that the Soviet Union hand back the Baltic territories.

Kristina set on a shelf the family photographs that she had carried on all their journeyings. The faces of the relatives they had left behind gazed back at them. They had no news of them and there was no way to get any. They could only pray that they had survived. Both Kristina and Lukas worried about their mothers and feared they might not see them again. The lack of communication was one of the hardest things to bear and always had been. It was like living in a pocket of air surrounded by fog, knowing that the world lay outside but being unable to see it.

In the place of pride, right in the center of the photographs, Kristina put Hugo. She looked at him levelly, without flinching. "I shall never give up hope."

"You are very strong, Mother," said Astra, who felt tears beginning to threaten and had to will herself to hold them back. "You and Father, both."

"And Olga and Paulis, too." Kristina looked somber for a moment, remembering the death of Paulis's mother and how they'd had to bury her in a field beside the railway track. "Is there not even a cemetery?" Paulis had asked in desperation. But all the cemeteries were full. They had made a rough wooden cross and inscribed her name on it—Elvira Jansons—and stuck it in the ground and Pastor Vizulis had said a few words. They had not been able to delay: the train had been waiting to set off again.

"We've all had to be strong," said Kristina. "You children, also! You've done well." She smiled and ruffled the top of Astra's head the way she sometimes did Tomas's—her daughter stood level with her now. "Your childhood came to rather an abrupt end, didn't it, love? Now then, let's give our new home a good clean-up!"

While Astra was sweeping the outside landing, the door of the next apartment opened and a girl came out. She looked two or three years younger than Astra. They said hello to one another.

Astra frowned. "I know you, don't I? You're Lora—Lora Berzins?"

"Yes! Are you Astra—Astra Petersons?"

They had been neighbors in Riga, had not seen each other for five years.

"You remember my brother Markus, don't you?" Lora turned to call back into the apartment. "Markus, the Petersons are here!"

Markus came at once. He had grown tall, was almost six feet.

"I wouldn't have known you," said Astra, laughing. They had started kindergarten together.

"You have not changed so much," said Markus.

"I don't know whether to take that as a compliment or not!"

"Oh, as a compliment."

"Are your parents with you?"

He sobered. "Our mother, only. Father was taken away by the Blue Hats in 1940. We've never heard what happened to him."

"I'm sorry. Very sorry."

"Did you all come through?"

"We lost Hugo."

Markus put out his hand and gripped hers. He did not have to speak.

All the refugees in their complex were Latvian. It was the only language to be heard on the stairs and in the courtyards. In all, there were twelve thousand Latvians in Eslingen in three different sites. This Lukas found out when he struck up a conversation with a high-ranking American officer, who told him also that Latvian schools were to be set up. Lukas hoped that he might be employed as a teacher of classics.

The officer said that they had had no idea that there would be all these nationalities to make provision for when the war ended—Baltic peoples, Poles, Czechs, Hungarians, Ukranians, Yugoslavs. Few wanted to go back to their own countries now that they were under Russian occupation. The Soviets were in control of all of eastern Europe. And then there were the millions of Germans who had been evacuated from the cities and wanted to go back to their homes, half of which were no longer standing. Not to mention the seven million or so prisoners-of-war! It was estimated that around twenty million Germans were homeless, apart from the other refugees. Even to provide the minimum of food and shelter for all of them was an immense task.

"But twelve thousand Latvians!" said Astra. "Surely one of them would have seen Hugo somewhere."

Lists of people trying to track down missing relatives were

being drawn up and circulated. Hugo's name was not among the ones they saw, but they presumed there might be others that had not come their way. Their distribution could not be foolproof considering the haphazard lines of communication that existed.

"We must make our own inquiries," said Lukas, "and be systematic about it." They would go from door to door with a photograph of Hugo and ask each person, "Have you seen this boy? Have you any news of a Hugo Petersons?" The refugees would have come from many different camps and traveled many different routes to get here.

They began with their own block. At each apartment, they were invited to come in and to partake of whatever refreshment could be offered. Among the tenants they found several old friends from Riga days and numerous acquaintances. Lukas met up with a number of his former students. Most visits lasted an hour or more. They heard tales that were similar to their own, of being shuttled around Germany and Poland, from one camp to another, and of loss. Many people had lost relatives, either through death or through separation.

"It will take a long time to get around all the Latvians," said Lukas, "but that cannot be helped." How could they brush aside the story of someone's tragedy? Everyone wanted to talk, to go over and over their experiences. It was better that way, said Lukas. Astra hoped that wherever Hugo was—if he still *was*—that he had found someone to whom he could talk. He had tended to bottle his troubles up inside himself until the pressure would build like steam inside a kettle and then the lid would fly off and he would explode. It was she who used to pick up the pieces. And now he would be on his own, whereas she still had Mother and Father and Tomas, as well as the Jansons. How lonely he must be!

In one apartment they came across a family who had lived near their country house in Latvia. They greeted one another warmly and talked for a long time. They came around to talking about Klavins and his son.

"I expect they will have been taken away to Siberia by now," said Mr. Zarins sadly.

"To Siberia?" cried Astra. "But why would anyone want to take them away?"

"They were landowners."

"They owned only a few acres. They weren't rich."

"I don't think you'd need to own much to be blacklisted, you know that, Lukas! And then Valdis was a member of the Farmers Union."

Astra and her father left soon afterward.

"Could it be true?" she asked her father. "That they might have taken Klavins and Valdis?"

"It's possible, I'm afraid."

She felt the tears coming.

"Cry!" her father said. "Don't be ashamed to cry."

As the American officer had predicted, schools were opened for the refugees. Tomas and Zigi went to the junior one, Astra and Mara to the high school where Lukas was taken on to teach languages, ancient and modern, and Kristina, art. The headmaster was an old friend of Lukas's from Riga days; they had been high school students together. Paulis acquired the position of head janitor. They were paid in kind for their services, with food and cigarettes, which could be traded on the black market.

The high school had been a German school; it was three-storied, brick, with an elegant facade, and set in the middle of a park. They walked there in the mornings, crossing first an old stone bridge over the Neckar, guarded by an ancient tower, and then they went through the small streets and alleys, which were permeated by the faint smell of cider. Apples and grapes were pressed there, right in the middle of the town. Markus and Lora usually joined the Petersons and Jansons.

Several of the children's old teachers had turned up, from Riga and from the school near their country home. They all found some former friends among their classmates, though the fate of many others was not known. Books were scarce, but gradually, from various places, they came trickling through. They were shared, passed around, copied. There was a general feeling of wanting to catch up, make good the time they had lost. They had no expectations of the world owing them a living because of their sufferings.

"People tire of other people's sorrows after a while," said Lukas. "We will not gain by harping on about our losses."

Their teachers comprised a number of former university professors, apart from Lukas. Standards were high. Science subjects were difficult without materials and had to be taught as theory. They had to take their teachers' word that the experiments they described worked.

A few of the refugees were lucky enough to find employment, some with the Americans, but most did not, and for them courses were run on a wide range of subjects, from bee-keeping to cobbling, plumbing, or tailoring. They knew they had to be prepared to learn new skills if they wanted to go to the countries of the New World. And if they could not go back to Latvia that was what they hoped to do.

Art clubs were also organized—one was run by Kristina—and singing and drama clubs, which put on highly accomplished performances in the school assembly hall. In them amateurs played alongside professional musicians and actors and actresses who had performed on the stage in Riga. Markus and Lora's mother had been an opera singer.

The school hall was used for many things, Boy Scout and Girl Guide meetings, and for religious services on Sunday. On the eighteenth of November, Latvian Independence Day, a huge parade marched to the school carrying banners and the red and white Latvian flag. Tomas and Zigi walked in the parade in their Cub outfits. Uniforms had been engineered by the women from whatever material was available.

The boys found life in Esslingen much to their liking. They were seldom in the apartment. When not at school they were running or jumping, or throwing or kicking balls. The men, under the supervision of Paulis, built a sports compound on a piece of waste ground that had previously been a rubbish dump. They labored long and hard, helped by swarms of excited children, until they had completed a shortened soccer field, four volleyball courts, and a sunken basketball court with seats for spectators carved into the hillside. The seats were made from wood salvaged from old orange crates.

Horseshoe pitching became a craze. The Americans came by in a truck one day and delivered a huge load of horseshoes to the complex—though no horses! Strange things were often given to the refugees; they had become used to that. On arrival, every man, woman, and child had received a pack containing four shaving brushes, four wristwatch straps (though no watches), and a leather belt.

Astra and Mara had each made new friendships and renewed old ones since coming to Esslingen, but remained best friends. They had sworn to be best friends always. Most things they did together. They had some interests that were different—Mara like to bake and sew, Astra preferred to read—but they shared many enthusiasms, which included the singing of Latvian national songs and American pop music. Markus had a radio, and a crowd of young people would squash into his room to hear the U.S. Armed Forces radio station. They sat on the floor, entranced, listening to the Hit Parade. For the next week the top ten would be heard on the apartment stairs and in the school playground. "It's been a long, long time from May to September..." "You are my sunshine, my only sunshine, you make me happy when skies are gray..."

The Latvians stayed very much within their own community and had little to do with the Germans, who resented them eating the food they grew and living in houses and apartments that had previously belonged to them. It was understandable, said Lukas. The shortage of food was still severe throughout Germany, particularly in the cities, where it was said that people were on the brink of starvation and small children were dying from malnutrition. In the country it was a little easier, with access to farm produce. Having little or no income, the refugees were given food, clothing, and housing free, by UNRA—the United Nations Relief Agency—whereas the native Germans were having a struggle to buy anything with the virtually worthless mark. Not much could be bought for money; most trade was done by barter. Exchange shops were set up and black marketeering was rife and conducted openly. Everyone participated. Some goods came on the black market through the people who worked for the Americans and some through the American soldiers themselves.

The Petersons and Jansons were skilled at survival, knew as well as anyone how to operate on the black market. Each week they put aside the chocolate from their food ration and some of the commodities earned at school, and the boys combed the American refuse dumps as they had done during the war, finding amazing things. Outside one camp the rubbish was labeled: EDIBLE GARBAGE, INEDIBLE GARBAGE, and TRASH ONLY. Once a month, Lukas and Paulis would load up rucksacks with shaving brushes, leather belts, cigarettes, chocolate, and anything the boys had scavenged, and disappear into the hills for the day, returning at nightfall with their sacks full of apples and pears, cheese and eggs and, on very rare occasions, a chicken.

Sometimes some of the Latvian boys would stray into other parts of town and end up in fist fights with their German contemporaries. Tomas and Zigi came home with split lips and black eyes.

"How many times do I have to tell you to stay away from places where there might be trouble?" asked Lukas.

"They call us names!" said Tomas.

"You must go near enough to hear them!"

"They say we're cowards because we ran away from our country," said Zigi. "We say they are because they lost the war!"

"It would be better to keep your mouths closed," said his father.

"Such a state of affairs is not particularly good," said Lukas, who did what he could to bridge the gap. He made a point of trying to engage Germans in conversation wherever he went and before long had several friends in Esslingen, classical scholars mainly. With one, he played chess regularly. But even so, he recognized that they would never really belong there, that they could not expect to be accepted as full members of the community. "We can never be Germans. So we will remain DPs. Displaced persons! That is why we cannot stay indefinitely."

"But where will we belong?" asked Astra. "If we can't go home. Do *you* think we shall?"

"I doubt it. I don't believe the Russians will let go of our country. They never have in the past without force. Why should they now?"

"Will we be DPs forever and ever, then?"

"We might get a chance to go to North America, or Australia, or New Zealand." The refugees pored over atlases, which showed that these places were a long way from Europe. On the other side of the world. They were foreign lands with different cultures, English-speaking.

In English classes pupils were exhorted to work hard. The language was one that everyone was going to need. Tomas and Zigi practiced on American soldiers whom they still followed about, picking up cigar butts and hoping for chewing gum. Memphis, Tennessee, and Dallas, Texas, crept into the boys' vocabulary. Zigi wanted to go to Texas and get a big hat. "It's called a Stetson and it's ten gallons!"

"I think I might like to go to Canada," said Kristina, who had been reading about it. "It sounds peaceful and there's lots of space."

"For now, anyway," said Lukas, "we have a home and food in our stomachs and the chance to recover our strength."

They were all putting some flesh back on their bones and Olga was being given iron injections by an American army doctor; and the boys had started to grow again. For a while they had seemed not to, and their legs had become a little bowed from lack of calcium. So everything was looking up—except for one thing. Hugo.

Astra and Lukas had continued with their search—it took several weeks to make the complete rounds. On the last evening that they went out, they found a woman who recognized Hugo from the photograph. She thought she had seen him in Gdynia, was convinced that she had.

"Yes, yes, I am sure I saw him! At the trains. It's the eyeglasses, you see. He had them knocked off in the crowd. They went flying over my head."

Astra covered her mouth with her hands. That was one of the things she had feared. How many times had she seen it happening in her mind's eye! She let her hands drop back down into her lap.

"He would be blind without his glasses," she said, turning to her father.

"What happened then?" Lukas asked the woman. "Can you remember? Did you see what he did?"

"I remember thinking, poor boy! And I looked around to see what was happening and then the crowd swept me on. You know how it was!"

Lukas nodded. "So you did not see him get on a train?"

"No, I did not. I am sorry I cannot help you any more."

Lukas thanked her and then he and Astra left. They went for a walk through the narrow streets of the old town. A light, gentle rain was falling. The winter was proving exceptionally mild—a blessing for those who had no heat in their homes. The streetlights cast pools of yellow between the old stone buildings. They had become fond of the town. Carol singers were singing somewhere near by, as they might have done at any time down the centuries, their voices rising up above the pantiled roofs into the still air. It would soon be Christmas. The second Christmas that they would spend without Hugo.

"Perhaps he never did leave Gdynia," said Astra. "Perhaps he is still there."

"He might well be," said her father. He sounded tired. And, for once, discouraged. Astra slipped her hand through the crook of his arm to help him along. His leg always dragged badly when he was fatigued, though he would never complain. He spoke of the benefit for others to talk out their problems but refused to burden anyone with his own. "If Hugo is still in Gdynia we have little chance of finding him. We must face up to that, Astra. It's a place we cannot go to or even communicate with. It's part of the Soviet bloc, just as Latvia is. And as we know only too well, a curtain has fallen between us and them. The Iron Curtain, I believe they are calling it."

In the late spring and early summer of 1946, they had news that raised their hopes, falsely. Lukas had written to the mayors of all the major cities in West Germany, asking if there were any Latvian refugees in their area. That way, they acquired a list of addresses where Latvians were being billeted. Painstakingly, Lukas had then written to each of them. From one, near Munich, a letter had come saying that the writer had heard of a boy called Hugo Petersons, an orphan, who was living in an apartment house with some others in a suburb of the city.

On the following Saturday, Lukas and Astra traveled to Munich, arriving at midday. They took a bus out to the suburb, which once would have been the sole territory of the wealthy. The house they were looking for must have been requisitioned, as their apartments had been. There was no one at home. They peered through the windows, saw signs of habitation: dishes on a table, an unmade bed, books. Astra thought she was going to be sick with the suspense. Olga had made them food for their journey, but they were unable to eat. They waited all afternoon outside the house, sitting on the pavement in the warm sunshine, until the first tenant came back. He was a Latvian boy, about eighteen years old. They told him why they were there.

"You're looking for Hugo? He said that his parents had been killed in a bombing raid."

Astra felt hope die in her, except for one small spark. Hugo might have *thought* they were killed. He might have heard that their train had been bombed. Many had been.

The boy, Olaf, invited them in. Others began to return. Ten young people lived in the house; they had all lost their relatives. Again, Astra and her father listened to their stories, Lukas asking questions from time to time, always gentle, always interested, always able to offer sympathy. At one point, when one of the boys began to weep for his lost parents, Astra had to get up and go outside: the weight of so much suffering was threatening to choke her. Hugo could well be sitting in another, similar house, somewhere, weeping for them.

She walked along the street, going as far as the corner, where she stood with her back against the trunk of a linden tree, watching the play of light and shadow as the branches moved in the breeze. The new leaves were fresh and green and smelled sweet. She lifted her arm and saw the patterning of sun and shade flicker over her skin. She thought of Hugo and Valdis and then of Markus, with whom she now spent quite a lot of time. They walked by the river together, talked for hours and hours about the past and the future, listened to his radio, went swimming. Mara said she was being disloyal to Valdis, that she should keep his memory green. "Your thoughts might reach out to him in Latvia or Siberia, if he *is* there, and comfort him. I expect he still thinks of you, Astra." Astra had to accept that that might well be true. Part of her hoped that he did, another that he did not. Her thoughts were full of confusion.

Mara's head seemed to be much clearer and her face was serene. She never doubted that they would find Hugo. "But you can't really be sure of that," Astra had said one day when she had been irritated by the reproachful look in her friend's eyes. Astra felt guilty that she did not have Mara's strong faith. She felt guilty when she let despair about Hugo overwhelm her. She had confessed it to her mother.

"Everyone copes in different ways, dear. Your mood vacillates—that is how you are. Mara's nature is to be like a rock."

"And I'm shifting sand!"

"Not at all! If you were you'd have been blown away by the wind by this time! It is just that Mara copes by refusing to allow the possibility of Hugo being lost for good even to enter into her consciousness. But I daresay that she has doubts about all sorts of things, deep down."

Looking around, Astra saw a boy with brown hair and glasses coming up the road. He had his hands in his pockets, and books under his arm. He was heading for the refugee house.

Instinctively she knew who he was—the other Hugo Petersons. The wrong one.

12

ANOTHER BIRTHDAY came around for Hugo—his seventeenth. He had been living with the Schneiders for almost three years now and spoke German fluently, with scarcely any trace of an accent. It was the only language that he used, apart from English, which he was studying in class. There were no other Latvians in the school or in the immediate area. He had heard that some were living in Hamburg, but he seldom went to the city and he felt disinclined to seek them out. If he did it would only open old wounds that he had done his best to close up and seal over. He had done everything that he could to put the past behind him and to live in the present. He had even begun to think in German, though he dreamed always in Latvian.

He still had dreams from which he would awake sweating and disoriented. In them often he would be running, fleeing, through a gray, formless landscape. He never arrived at a destination. He would sit up in the box bed, his heart pounding as if he had been running, and stare into the shadows of the room. The light reflected from the stove flickered over the rag rug, the faded cloth upholstery of the armchairs, the china on the dresser. He would see then that he was in the Schneiders' kitchen. And his bedroom. The other room, with the wood floor and open casement window, that sometimes appeared on the edge of a dream was no longer a part of his life and never could be again.

He had come to think of the Schneiders as his family and of their house as his home. "I must be getting home," he would say when he took leave of Doctor Braun. His conscious mind acknowledged that his home was here; it was his unconscious that kicked against it, throwing up those fitful dreams of rootlessness and homelessness.

He still had thoughts of being a doctor. In two years' time, in 1949, when he became nineteen, he would graduate from secondary school, after which he would begin his medical training at the university in Hamburg. The system would allow him to attend whatever classes he could, and fit in a part-time job around them. It meant that it might take him a little longer to qualify—six and a half years perhaps, or seven, instead of six. The Schneiders were happy to have him continue living with them during that time.

"We want you to get a good education," said Herr Schneider.

Hugo was already working on weekends and during school holidays on a local farm. The farmer paid in produce, which Hugo contributed to the household. Frau Schneider said he would run himself into the ground.

"You don't have time for other things! It is all work, work, and more work, Hugo!"

"The farm work's good for me. It gives me fresh air and exercise and helps to balance my studies, does it not?" He smiled and so, too, did she, for the length of time he spent hunched over his books vexed her. She found it difficult not to harangue him. He would ruin his eyes, and then what? His eyes were not strong to begin with, were they? But he must read, he would reply, in order to study, and that would end the exchange, for the present.

Often he would work until late into the night, long after the others had gone to bed, when there was only the crackle of the fire and the occasional hoot of an owl or rustle of some other night animal to disturb the silence. He had always liked the feeling of being awake while others slept. Night owl, Astra used to call him and then she'd make a hooting noise, batting her fingers against her mouth. When he felt at peace he tried to think of her and not to banish her from his mind. Putting the past behind him did not mean denying it altogether or forgetting his family. The difficulty lay in getting the balance right between remembering and forgetting.

Bettina started work at the farm, also. On Saturday mornings they would rise at five and walk through the dark lanes to the farmstead. They liked to watch the first streaks of pink and turquoise and pale lemon edging into the eastern sky and the trees and hedges beginning to take shape around them. They listened to the chirpings of the early birds.

"It's as if no one was awake in the whole world but us and the birds," said Bettina. "You feel you should walk on tiptoe in case you disturb anything."

Hugo inhaled deeply. "It does smell fresh and untrodden, doesn't it?" It was difficult to think that armies had fought over this land and bombs had rained from the sky, tearing great jagged holes in the earth and flattening habitations.

The farmer usually set them to work together at the various jobs, picking potatoes and turnips, hoeing, mucking out the barns, haying. Bettina liked to talk while she worked and did not mind Hugo's silences or even that sometimes when she was telling him a story about Hilde or someone in the village he would not be listening fully. "Uhuh," he would say or nod, but his mind would be far away, on physics or biology or Aristotle. Or in Latvia. But she thought that he dwelled on that less than he used to. The curtain of darkness swept across his face less often now. Her father said it would take time for Hugo's grief to heal, and they must allow him that. "He's doing everything that he can to make a life for himself here." Herr Schneider hoped that one day when Hugo was a qualified doctor he might become a German citizen. It would be easier for him to make headway in his profession if he did.

Bettina herself was going to train as a nurse. The Schneiders were pleased: the lives of their two young were shaping up satisfactorily. "And perhaps, who can tell," said Frau Schneider to her husband, "they might be able to work together one day. Wouldn't that be splendid!"

In the late autumn Doctor Braun had become increasingly frail, was troubled with recurring bouts of bronchitis, and came down with an attack of pleurisy. He was taken to the hospital in Hamburg.

Hugo went daily to visit him. He did not need to ask the doctor in charge to know that his friend was unlikely to recover. It showed on every line of the old man's face. Hugo sat for hours beside the bed while Doctor Braun slept.

Every now and then the patient would wake and they would talk a little, Hugo having to incline his head and listen closely to make out the faint voice.

"Don't fret when I'm gone, Hugo. Promise!"

"I'll try not to."

"I've left you all my books, lad, and my notebooks and stethoscopes. Everything in my study is yours."

"Thank you." Hugo put his warm hand over the cold papery one. For everything, he added, and went on to tell Doctor Braun how much his friendship had meant to him, something he had wanted to do before, but had never been able to find the words. "The light in your study has been like a beacon to me. When I came through the village and saw it shining up ahead, I would start to run!"

A smile flickered over the doctor's face. "Good luck, Hugo. You will make a fine doctor."

Hugo had seen death often before but he was deeply moved when he saw the life go out of this old man's face. He took off his glasses and wept. But when a nurse came in and he got up to go, he was quite calm.

Bettina was waiting for him in the corridor. She looked at his face, then she took his hand and led him out. They walked to the Auszenalster, the big lake in the center of the city. The autumnal air was crisp, the lake blue under a blue sky, the trees aflame with reds and oranges. Hugo saw that it was a beautiful day. Intensely beautiful. Death heightened life: that was something he had already learned. He remembered Sergei, the young Russian soldier who had died in his arms. It had been the first time he had seen someone die, but it had not frightened him as much as he would have expected, though it had affected him greatly, and saddened him.

They stopped beside the lake and gazed down into the water, at the reflections of the trees. They saw their own reflections, too, shimmering a little, side by side, close together.

"You'll miss Doctor Braun, won't you, Hugo?" said Bettina softly.

Hugo nodded. "But he was ready to go and it would be selfish of me to wish that he hadn't. Though at the moment I do feel selfish. Very selfish!"

Bettina laid a hand on his arm and he turned to her.

"What would I do without you, Betti?"

She smiled, and the dimples deepened in her cheeks.

They had not gone with the passing of adolescence. He touched one with the tip of his finger.

"Your face shines, did you know that? You are like a sunflower."

She blushed and bent her head slightly, pushing a strand of golden-yellow hair behind her ear. He lifted her chin with his hand, looked into her face and then kissed her.

Soon afterward, Frau Braun sold the house and went to live with her sister in Bonn. The contents of the doctor's study were delivered to the Schneiders' door: books—hundreds, thousands of books—stethoscopes, boxes of thermometers, syringes, hypodermic needles, bandages, dusty bottles containing substances whose names were fading on the yellowed labels. Everything was dusty. Frau Schneider sneezed violently as she bent to examine them.

"Where are we to put all this stuff? Our three little rooms are already packed."

It was true: there was not much space left among the furnishings. And the loft was full of bits of rolled-up linoleum, old carpets, blankets, tools. Frau Schneider was thrifty, had never thrown anything out since her marriage.

"We'll have to find somewhere for it, Mother," said Bettina.

"No, it's not possible to keep it all," said Hugo. "I'll sort out the things I want and try to sell the rest."

"You must keep everything you think you might need," said Bettina. "You can put some of it in my room."

They stowed boxes under her bed and stacked books against the walls, once Frau Schneider had dusted them thoroughly. She would not allow her daughter to sleep with all that dust in the air! Of course the Brauns had been very old and unable to keep their place in a proper way, but she liked a house to be clean and smell sweet. The musty smell of the books was not as easy to banish as the dust. There was just enough room for Bettina to squeeze around her door and crawl into the bed, but that did not bother her. She was hardly ever in the room except to sleep; all life at the Schneiders took place in the kitchen.

Herr Schneider took some of the newer, less pungent-smelling books and put them under his and his wife's bed. A few others found a space in the loft.

"Some day, Hugo, when you're a fully qualified doctor, you'll have a study as big as Doctor Braun's and arrange them all on shelves again!" said Bettina.

The remainder of the books Hugo took to Hamburg. Hilde's boyfriend, Heinz, borrowed his father's car—his father was reputed to be a big operator on the black market and to have plenty of money—and drove him into town one afternoon after school. Hilde and Bettina went along for the ride.

The city was still gathering itself together from the wartime bombings. Much of the rubble had been bulldozed away and squares stood leveled to the ground, waste spaces that the wind howled across, where stray, half-wild dogs scavenged. Some streets had started to rise again. But there were homeless people who were squatting yet in cellars and old raid shelters. They passed a woman begging with a rheumy-eyed child and a man sitting on the pavement with a patch over one eye and an empty trouser leg pinned up.

A few secondhand booksellers had set up in business again, operating from dusty backstreet premises. The first one they tried was scornful. "Out-of-date textbooks are not much use to anybody! They'd hardly earn a pfennig! I am supposed to be making a living. I cannot even afford to feed my family." The next one picked through the boxes and agreed to buy half the books for a small amount. It was better than nothing.

There remained the problem of what to do with the rest of the books. Hugo could not bring himself to dump or burn them and yet they could not be allowed to return to clutter up Frau Schneider's kitchen. Heinz said he would talk his father into letting them be stored in the back of their garage.

"So that settles that," said Hilde. "Now let's go to a café! And then perhaps we could go to a film."

In the café they drank coffee that tasted as if it had been made from dandelion leaves, which it probably had, but it was agreeable just to sit at a table by the window and talk and watch the world go by.

"I love cafés," said Hilde. "My mother says that the cafés before the war were fantastic! You could get real coffee from Brazil—even the smell was enough to make you swoon!—and they had cakes made with cream and chocolate and almonds."

"Don't, Hilde!" Bettina protested. "You're making me hungry."

They drank two cups of coffee apiece and shared two slices of carrot cake, then they went to a cinèma. Hugo spent almost half of the money he'd made on the books, but he did not mind. It was necessary to spend money on enjoyment, too, at times: that was what his father used to say.

Sometimes, on Sundays, the Schneiders would go for a meal to a nearby inn, after Bettina and Hugo had returned from their work at the farm. Many of the locals had the habit of going to the inn on Sundays. The food, which was acquired with coupons from their ration books, was simple but wholesome enough: there might be potatoes and red cabbage and perhaps sausage. The atmosphere was warm and lively. Hugo found that he looked forward to these outings. It was a time in the week when he could unwind completely and forget about studying or having to scrimp and save money. An accordionist would play and some of the young ones would get up and dance.

"Come on, Hugo!" Bettina did not allow him to sit.

Laughing, protesting, he would take her outstretched hand and go. They laughed a lot as they danced and Bettina would make exaggerated faces whenever he trod on her toe.

"They look well together, the two of them, do they not?" said Frau Schneider to her husband as they watched them waltz past, their arms around each other's waists.

"Very well." Herr Schneider sipped his beer contentedly.

"They are fond of one another, I think."

Herr Schneider nodded. "He is a fine young man."

In January, Bettina celebrated her eighteenth birthday by becoming betrothed to Hugo.

"I know I'm young—not eighteen myself yet—but we would like to be betrothed," said Hugo. "Even though we might have to wait some years to marry."

"You're very mature for your age, Hugo," said Herr Schneider. "And that is what counts. Your life has been hard and has taught you much. We would be very happy to have you for our son-in-law one day."

"It has been our dearest wish," said Frau Schneider and came forward to kiss Hugo on both cheeks.

13

LUKAS wrote about two thousand letters—they lost count—to places in different parts of the world: Britain, Canada, the United States, Australia, New Zealand. He wrote to mayors of towns and cities, heads of universities, and schools. He wrote on behalf of himself and his friend Paulis Jansons, explaining their situation, asking for employment and accommodation. They would need both before they would be allowed to leave Germany and become immigrants in a new country. Once they had those guarantees, their passages to that country would be paid by the International Relief Organization.

Writing the letters, researching first where to send them, occupied most of Lukas's evenings, and the materials—notepaper, envelopes, pen nibs, bottles of ink, stamps—had to be bartered for.

He was well known at the local post office.

"More letters for abroad, Herr Petersons!" said the postmistress. "Your arm must be aching."

Some of his colleagues at school thought he was crazy.

"Who's going to give a Latvian DP a job, sight unseen, with an apartment thrown in?"

Paying no attention, Lukas persisted with his efforts.

Whenever he wrote to a new place, they would look it up on the map and consider the pros and cons. The North Island or the South Island in New Zealand? The South was nearer the South Pole, said Astra, and so would be colder; she would like to go somewhere warm. Which would be better—the east or the west coast of the United States?

Everyone had a favorite place that he thought about and pictured going to. They daydreamed a lot, fully aware that they would not have this choice in reality; they were playing a game. They knew that they would be lucky to be offered anything. Astra and Mara had long conversations about life in New York, San Francisco, Sydney, Toronto, New Orleans. Knowing little about any of these cities was not a deterrent to talking about them. Magazines from abroad were passed from hand to hand until they fell into tatters.

The postman was eagerly awaited. Some days he carried sheafs of letters in his hand for them. About half of the people written to replied. There was much excitement as each envelope was opened, although after a while that gave way to a kind of resignation, to an expectation that the letter would say no. They usually began with the words, "I am very sorry I am unable to help you. . . ." They were sympathetic, and some were able to offer jobs, but it was the accommodation that was the sticking point. Eventually all the refugees who wanted to go would probably be helped to emigrate under an official scheme, but that would mean arriving jobless, dependent on handouts, perhaps even living in camps again. They were tired of being at the receiving end, wanted to take their lives into their own hands.

Lukas refused to give up. They must be patient and perhaps someone, somewhere, would be able and willing to help them. Some refugees had relatives abroad who were prepared to stand as guarantors for them, but the Petersons and the Jansons had no one. The Berzins had relatives in both the States and Britain and were hoping to go to one or the other.

One morning in May 1948, a letter came from Boston, Massachusetts, offering Paulis a job as janitor at a high school, with an apartment included. The headmaster was Polish, he had gone to America in the early thirties, knew what it was like to leave one's homeland and make a life in a new country. He said that he would be very happy to welcome Paulis and his family and to sign all the necessary forms.

They rushed at once for the atlas. The state of Massachusetts was on the east coast of America, they saw, and Boston was on the sea, looking over the Atlantic Ocean.

"You would enjoy being so near the sea," said Lukas. In Esslingen, they felt landlocked. They had not seen the sea since they had made their terrible journey down through the Baltic Sea into the Gulf of Danzig.

"But there is no job for you there," said Paulis unhappily.

The headmaster had written that he would have liked to have been able to help Lukas also, but regretted he had no accommodation to offer for teachers.

"You must take it, Paulis," Lukas told him. "You can't afford to turn down the chance."

"But the families would be split up." Olga sounded stunned.

"We can't let that happen!" said Astra.

"No, we can't." Mara was close to tears.

"I'm not leaving Tom," declared Zigi. "I'm staying here!"

"We have to be realistic," said Lukas, "and accept the fact that it will be exceedingly difficult to find accommodation *and* jobs for both families in the same place."

"I'm sick of being realistic!" cried Astra. "I'm sick of having to accept. Sick, sick, sick!"

Her father fell silent.

"I'm sorry, Father, I shouldn't have shouted at you." She went to him and laid her head against his shoulder. In these four years he had aged, his face had grown thin, and his beard was streaked with white.

"It's all right, dear—I understand. Sometimes I want to shout myself!"

Kristina said, "Perhaps there is no need to make any decision straight away. I think we should let the idea settle awhile."

Paulis nodded. "You're right, Kristina. We mustn't rush into anything too quickly. After all, it is our whole future that is at stake."

Two weeks later a letter came from a high school in Toronto offering Lukas a job. One of the members of the staff, who was himself half-Latvian on his mother's side, was willing to let the Petersons live on the top floor of his house. "It is a big old house," the headmaster wrote, "and there are only three rooms on the top floor, but perhaps you would be able to manage until you find something better? At least it is a base for you to come to, and I know that the owner, Ivar Fraser, would make you most welcome."

They rushed at once to get the atlas to see how far Toronto was from Boston.

"It doesn't seem too far," said Tomas dubiously.

"It's a small-scale map," said Astra. "It must be several hundred miles and there's Lake Ontario in between." She began to measure with her finger. "It might be all right if you could fly from one place to the other, like a crow. But going by public transport would take ages. So I don't think *that's* on."

The parents were saying very little. Astra did not like the looks on their faces.

"You're not thinking of taking up the two offers, are you?"

"I don't think we have much choice, dear," said her mother. "I wish it weren't so, but—"

"Let's wait!" Astra pleaded. "Just a little while."

"We might end up waiting too long and losing these opportunities," said her father. "After all, they are the only two offers that we've had. And it's becoming more difficult for us to survive here."

He meant financially. The old, virtually worthless reichsmark had been replaced by the new Deutschemark, which had had an electric effect on the economy. Trading was now conducted with money again, goods had reappeared in the shops, and the black market had vanished more or less overnight. This was good for the Germans, not so good for the refugees who had no access to currency.

"And perhaps we'll find a way to be together again afterward," said Lukas. "I will try to get Paulis a job in Toronto. Once we have a house of our own we will have a place for them to come to."

They had made up their minds, Astra realized, as soon as they had opened the Toronto letter. After all the talking it now looked as if they were actually going to leave Europe and go to North America—the dream continent. Did she really want to go? It was a place that had seemed to belong only to dreams and glossy magazines and the music that they listened to on Markus's radio. But to go there would mean giving up any hope of ever returning to Latvia and of finding Hugo who, if he was still alive, must be on this continent somewhere. She could never go wholeheartedly while she did not know the fate of her twin. Her other half. Even after nearly four years she still felt the pain of their severance and that a part of her was missing. Going away would involve losing friends in Esslingen also—Markus and Lora and others.

She went for a walk by the river with Markus. The day was warm, the river sparkled, the countryside looked lush and green with the approach of mid-summer, the grapes were ripening on the vine. Summers were warmer and lusher here than they had been farther north in Latvia.

"I wouldn't mind so much staying in Germany," she said. "We've got our own place here."

"You don't want to be a DP forever though, do you? And live two families to one small apartment?"

"I suppose not." She sighed. "How about your plans?"

"We're still waiting to hear. My father's cousin in Wisconsin is trying to get papers through for us. So is my mother's cousin in Scotland."

"Which one will you go to?"

"It depends on which comes up first."

"Isn't it strange to think that one's destiny can be decided like that, as if by the flip of a coin?"

One by one, all the families would go, except for those who were unfortunate enough to have an invalid among them. No country would take anyone with tuberculosis or some other chronic illness. There was trade on the black market with chest X rays.

When Olga had her chest X rayed it was touch and go as to whether she would be passed. A slight shadow showed on the left lung. The doctor thought she had probably had a mild form of TB at some point. She had to be X rayed again. For days they lived through agony until she was declared clear enough.

Letters went to and fro between Esslingen and Boston and Toronto; it seemed that there were no snags at the other end. They were expected. Weeks passed as they awaited news of their transatlantic passages. And then letters came telling them that they were to sail in November from Cuxhaven, the Jansons for New York, and the Petersons for Quebec. They were to proceed first to a refugee camp outside Hamburg.

"Oh, Astra!" said Mara, taking her friend's hand and gripping it tightly. They looked into each other's faces.

"I expect Father will find a way to get you to Toronto. You know what he's like! Or perhaps we will come to Boston."

It had gone too far now for the decisions to be revoked; knowing that, they accepted the next step in their lives to be inevitable. They began to pack up.

They had a party on their last night in Esslingen. So many people came that they overflowed the apartment's boundaries onto the landing and stairs. Much cheap wine was drunk and many songs were sung. Afterward, Astra walked for half the night with Markus along the riverbank. It was a clear night and the sky was sprinkled with stars. They'd write, they promised, keep in touch, meet up in North America. To everyone she parted from she made the same promises. It was easy to make promises, of course, but it didn't look too far from Ontario to Wisconsin, did it? They were just across the Great Lakes from one another. Just! But perhaps it might be possible to take a steamer to go between the two places? And they would be able to earn the money to do these things, as Markus pointed out. They had heard that if you were prepared to work hard in North America you could be successful. Everyone was given a chance—even immigrants. Markus and Astra both wanted to go to college but knew that they would have to take jobs first to raise the money. Astra hoped to study languages. She had inherited her father's gift, was fluent in German, and could converse well in both English and French.

"I feel so ignorant about this place that we're going to," she said. "I can't begin to imagine it. Will it have skyscrapers, I wonder? Will the people be nice?"

In the morning a van came and the wooden crates containing their possessions were loaded onto it. Astra and Markus said good-bye casually, as if they expected to meet the following week. Astra had thought about it beforehand and decided that that was the way it had to be; she could not go through the same heart-wrenching parting that she had done with Valdis. She had been only fourteen then. Now she was eighteen and did not expect her relationship with Markus to be a lasting one, to survive separation and the taking on of a new life. The changes that were coming into their lives were monumental and would leave no time for looking over one's shoulder.

They traveled from Stuttgart to Hamburg by rail. They filled a compartment. Tomas and Zigi had brought with them a Latvian flag, which they jammed into the top of the open window. The red and white pennant fluttered in the breeze as the train whisked them northward up through Germany toward the North Sea. Mara and her mother were both knitting. It looked a soothing occupation and Astra wished that she were more adept at it herself. Her own efforts usually ended disastrously. Her mother was drawing. She had a collection of sketchbooks that charted their lives over the last four years. Browsing through them, Astra saw how the faces of herself and Mara and the boys had changed and matured. And Klara had grown from a baby into a little girl. Astra gazed briefly at Hugo, aged fourteen, frozen in time, then closed the sketchbook. Paulis, Zigi, and Tomas were playing cards. Lukas was reading a book, though Astra noticed that he seldom turned a page. She was the only one who seemed unable to settle to anything. She got up and went into the corridor.

She stood by an open window and allowed the breeze to cool her face and ruffle her hair. She watched the countryside as it flipped past, studded with trees and farms and houses. The leaves had turned on the trees and some branches were bare. It was autumn, the same time of year that they had made their first train journey as refugees, after arriving at Gdynia. She still remembered her feeling of sheer panic when she had realized that Hugo was not with them. He was in her thoughts throughout this journey, too.

When they were not far from Hamburg, the train stopped. Putting her head out of the window, she saw that they were waiting for a signal to change. A moment later it did and they crawled forward again. They drew level with the signal box. The signalman glanced down at her and smiled. He must have seen many refugees like us, she thought. He had a kind face. She waved to him and he lifted his hand in response. They were past now.

There was a path above the railway track and two people were walking on it, a boy and a girl. The boy had his arm around the girl's waist. The sight of them brought a pang to Astra's heart. She would miss Markus! In the last year they had become close. The girl on the path had curly golden-yellow hair that gleamed in the afternoon sunshine. She was laughing and looking up into the boy's face. The boy appeared vaguely familiar. Astra's heart began to flutter. And then the train picked up speed and with a whistle plunged into a tunnel.

Emerging from the other side into the light again, Astra told herself not to be so foolish. Of course it could not have been Hugo!

14

WALKING on the railway path with Bettina, Hugo watched the train pass.

"Look, Bettina!" he said excitedly, pointing. "I'm sure that was the Latvian flag. Did you see it?"

The carriage with the flag had gone now, into a tunnel. Bettina had not seen it; she had been looking at Hugo.

"I'm sure it was! It's striped red, white, and red, horizontally."

The sight of it had jolted him, reawakened old memories. That night he lay awake for a long time. During the next few days he kept thinking about it and one morning, at breakfast, said that he was going to catch the bus into Hamburg after school.

Bettina looked up in surprise. They had talked of going with Hilde to Heinz's house to listen to records.

"I have to take some books back to the library," said Hugo and at once felt guilty that he should have lied to her. Why had he? As he sat on the bus pondering it, he could not be sure. He thought he had not wanted to worry her. But what could there be for her to worry about just because he wanted to follow a Latvian flag? It was instinct that had made him put forward a screen to cover his activities. Perhaps it was that when he felt homesick for Latvia it seemed to imply that he did not feel at home with the Schneiders.

Being in a camp brought back to the families echoes of the ones they'd been in during the war—the communal living, the lack of privacy, the lumpy food. There was no war on now, of course, no planes buzzed overhead, no artillery fire could be heard at night; but still they felt uneasy and restless. The camp, an old army barrack, was dreary and soulless. Each morning they went to look at the bulletin board to see if their sailings were listed. The days dragged past. Their books were packed, they had tired of playing cards and word games and charades, and no one had as much to talk about as usual, not even Tomas and Zigi, who lapsed at times into silence. Tomas would take out his sketchbook and draw and Zigi would whittle away at a piece of wood that was gradually taking shape as a miniature canoe. Klara clung to her mother, sensing that something was up.

"It will be better when we are actually away," said Lukas to Astra. "When we are committed and know that there is no turning back. This hanging around is bad for everyone's nerves."

Astra felt that her nerves were as taut as piano wire. If anyone looked at her the wrong way or said the wrong thing, she twanged. She could feel the vibrations inside her head.

"Oh, shut up!" she snapped at Tomas one gray afternoon when he'd been prattling on about North America, as if it were going to be a paradise flowing with chewing gum, chocolate, and Uhu glue. "It's about time you grew up—who cares about glue, for goodness sake!"

She had to go for a walk to calm down. She knew she had

been unfair to Tomas: he had grown up in the last year and was wise and sensible for a twelve-year-old. He had had to learn to be. He took the rough with the smooth, did not complain or kick—the way she did! And when he had talked about the glories of Uhu and chewing gum he had been parodying himself as he had been when younger. He and Zigi had a good sense of fun and she had no right to try to kill it. When she got back she would tell him she was sorry. But she thought that he probably knew that already. Tomas was not stupid, even though he liked to caper and play the fool.

A bus was coming. She had a few marks in her pocket. On impulse, she jumped on board. It was going to Hamburg.

Hugo stopped in first at the library to change some books so that he would not have to lie again on his return. Doing so renewed his feeling of guilt. Then he went to the railway station.

A train with refugees? There were no such trains nowadays, he was told, but it was possible that refugees had been traveling on a regular scheduled service. Refugees of all nationalities were living in a camp outside the city while awaiting passage to the countries of the New World.

"They sail from Cuxhaven. There could be Latvians among them—you'd have to go yourself to check that."

Hugo thanked the man and asked if he could give him the address of the camp.

"I'm afraid I can't. But they'll be able to tell you at the post office."

Back on the street, Hugo stood undecided. Should he go? It was a long time since he had seen any of his countrymen. For the last three years he had done what he could to avoid them. But now he had a yearning to meet a fellow Latvian again, to talk with someone in his native tongue, who would understood his roots and background, who might know people and places he had known. Then again, the experience might be too unsettling. Could he afford to take that risk? No, he decided, he could not, not now that his life was going so well.

Astra got off in the center of the town and wandered around. A slight drizzle of rain had started to fall. It was getting colder. The year was moving on. They would start their new life on the American continent in winter. She pulled up the collar of her jacket.

There were a number of young people about. She glanced at them idly, wondering about their lives. Some looked like students. A boy was walking up ahead of her, carrying a stack of books under one arm. The back of his head looked familiar. And there was something about the way he walked. . . . Suddenly she remembered the boy on the railway path and her heart began to hammer. "Hugo!" she yelled. *"Hu—go!"*

Hearing his name, Hugo turned and saw a girl coming toward him, running, her shoulder-length fair hair flying out behind her. She was wearing shining yellow beads that swung to and fro as she ran. She was still calling his name. He felt himself begin to tremble. He dropped his books and went racing to meet her.

They collided and his glasses, knocked by the edge of Astra's hand, went soaring in an arc over their heads and landed on the pavement.

"Your glasses," gasped Astra.

"Doesn't matter," said Hugo, but she was already down on her knees recovering them.

She sat back on her haunches cradling them between her hands. "One of the lenses is cracked," she said, distressed.

He squatted down on the pavement in front of her. Passersby had to circle around them and some muttered objections about the thoroughfare being blocked, but the twins neither noticed nor heard. They stared at each other. She was blurred and fuzzy to him, but he would have known her blindfolded. To be close to her was enough. Even the sound of her breathing was familiar.

"It doesn't matter," he said again, taking the glasses from her and putting them on. "They can be mended." With the good eye he saw her wide gray eyes, the small freckles spattered across the bridge of her nose, her cheeks pink from running and excitement. She was four years older, but it was the same Astra. He put his arms around her neck to grasp her and they toppled over sideways onto the pavement, laughing and crying.

"I can't believe it!" she kept saying.

"I thought you were dead! I thought you'd been killed in Leipzig. What about Mother and Father and Tomas?"

"They're well!"

"Thank God!"

"And the Jansons?"

"They're all right, too. Except for Granny—she died on one of our journeys."

"Poor old Granny Jansons."

"Oh, Hugo, it's like a miracle—finding you! But it's true enough, isn't it? It's really *you*? I'm not dreaming? I've dreamed about you so much."

"Pinch me!" he said and she did, weakly, shaking her head, laughing, wiping away the tears with her forearm.

He put out his hand and touched her amber beads. "Grandmother's necklace!"

She put out her hand and touched the jagged scar that zigzagged from his temple down onto his cheek.

"I got that in Gdynia."

"You must tell me."

"Let's go and have some coffee!" He helped her up. Her legs felt as if they were filled with jelly.

It was dark by the time they emerged from the coffeehouse. They had so much to talk about! How would they ever catch up? It would take weeks, months, said Astra, and even in the years to come they might stop and say, Did I ever tell you about the time when . . . ?

They took a bus out to the camp. They said little on the short ride, both emotionally worn out.

Astra led Hugo through the camp to the hut where the Petersons and Jansons lived and slept. Outside the door, she motioned to him to wait. She went in alone.

"Astra," said her mother, looking up from her sketchbook, "there you are! We were getting worried."

"Are you all right?" asked her father, frowning. "You look—"

"Hugo is here," she blurted out, although she had meant to break the news slowly.

"*Hugo*?" The book slipped from her mother's lap.

There was silence in the room.

Lukas said, "Astra, you wouldn't joke—?"

The door opened again and Hugo entered. His mother was first to move; she went to him and locked him in her arms, and then came Lukas to embrace him, and Tomas, and, in their turn, Olga, Paulis, Mara, and Zigi.

"Why is everyone crying?" asked Klara.

The Schneiders were not too worried when Hugo did not return by the five o'clock bus.

"You know what he's like once he gets his head in a book!" said Bettina.

At six, Frau Schneider was ready with their evening meal.

"Let's wait until the next bus is due," said Bettina.

They waited, and then they sat down at the table. Bettina had little appetite.

"I'm sure nothing can have happened to him," said Herr Schneider. "He's a full grown man now, after all."

"Still, there are bad parts in Hamburg," his wife pointed out.

"I doubt if Hugo would go into them."

"He's been a little—well, strange, recently," said Bettina hesitantly. "As if he were not fully here. He saw a flag on a train. Oh, I'm sure it can't be that!"

After the dishes had been washed she went to the village to see Hilde. Hilde's house was right beside the bus stop.

"She senses something is amiss," said Frau Schneider.

She went herself to stand at the door, to look out into the dark night. She was always the same when either of the two young ones was late home; she could never settle. There was nothing to be seen outside except for the slanting rain that shimmered in the yellow shaft of light falling from the doorway. She heard the whistle of a train in the distance. It sounded melancholy to her ears and she wondered that her husband had continued to enjoy the sight and sound of trains all these years. To her, trains meant leaving, going away. She had traveled little in her life, had never wanted to. She liked her home too much and hoped that when Bettina and Hugo married they would live nearby, in the village, perhaps, although Gustav said that she must be prepared for them wanting to live in Hamburg.

"Better come in, Grete. Standing there won't bring him any faster and the draft is making the stove smoke."

Bettina came home at half-past nine, after the last bus had arrived. Her head was wet and her eyes anxious. Her mother made her a hot drink of linden tea. At ten, which was when they normally went to bed, Herr Schneider wound the clock, stoked the stove, and locked the back door. His wife rinsed the cups and tidied the hearth. Then they sat down once more to wait.

It was almost midnight when Hugo came in. He stood, dripping wet, just inside the door, shaking water from his hair. One of the lenses of his eyeglasses was splintered with cracks.

"What happened, Hugo?" asked Frau Schneider.

"I found my family," he said.

Next morning, Lukas said he must move quickly if he were to try to arrange a passage for Hugo.

"But we don't know yet whether he will come with us or not," said Kristina in a quiet, subdued voice.

"Of course he will come!" said Astra. "How could he not?"

"There's this girl—"

"I had to say good-bye to Markus, didn't I?"

"This is different, Astra—they're betrothed and he has lived with her family for four years. They have been kind to him, more than kind—generous. *Very* generous. They took him in, a complete stranger—"

"He can't stay with them just because he feels grateful to them! Can he?"

No one answered Astra's question. Tomas began to bounce a ball against the wall.

"Don't do that, *please*, Tom," said his mother.

"I want Hugo to come with us," said Tomas.

"I know you do, dear. We all do."

Lukas went out, saying he was going to start making the

arrangements, anyway, so that if Hugo did want to come he would be able to.

"It might not be possible to get him an immediate passage, of course," said Kristina.

"Surely they'd let one more person on when he's part of a family that's already going," said Astra.

"I just don't want you to be too disappointed, love, if it doesn't work out."

"Disappointed? I'd be worse than disappointed—I'd be devastated!"

Astra and Mara took a load of dirty washing to the laundry. They worked in two sinks, side by side. Astra pummeled the clothes, sending sprays of water in all directions.

"He must be in love with—with Bettina," said Mara, finding the girl's name difficult to say. She felt as if she had a great big ball stuck at the back of her throat, lodged there since yesterday when Hugo had told them of his betrothal. She knew it was silly of her to feel so upset; she and Hugo had not seen each other for four years, and when last they had been together they had been children. He thought of her with affection, that was all, as if she were another sister.

"Ah, Mara," he had said, hugging her to him, "it's so good to see you! You haven't changed one little bit."

"I expect they're like brother and sister." Astra twisted a towel between her hands and wrung it out. "He and Bettina. Well, they must be, mustn't they, living under the same roof, being brought up together? I don't suppose he is in love with her."

"Why then is he betrothed to her?"

"Mara, people get married for all sorts of reasons, not just love. Sometimes it's just because someone is *there*. And he probably felt he had to, since the Schneiders had been so kind to him. They saved his life, after all, and that's a big debt to try to repay."

They carried the washing outside where they hung it on straggling ropes. It hung limply in the damp November air. Their towels were beginning to look really threadbare, Astra noticed; you could see the light through them in several places. They would seem pitiful to people who were used to buying new things whenever they needed them. Imagine being able to do that! They would certainly not be able to hang rags like this out in public when they got to Canada.

"Don't worry, Mara, I'm sure he won't stay. We've just found him, so it's not meant that we should lose him again so quickly."

The Schneiders invited the Petersons to visit them. Lukas, Kristina, and Astra went; Tomas decided to stay at home and play football with Zigi and the other boys.

Herr Schneider said that he was very happy to meet the family of Hugo. Lukas said that they were profoundly grateful to them for saving the life of their son and taking him into their home. He stressed their gratitude. "We can never repay you, Herr Schneider." "That is not necessary, Herr Petersons." Both men spoke formally. They were strangers, after all. Frau Schneider and Bettina stood shyly in the background. Astra stole a glimpse of Bettina, not wanting to meet her eye directly, not yet at least. She looked nice, and she was very pretty!

"My wife, Grete," Herr Schneider was saying, and Astra stepped forward to shake her hand. "And my daughter, Bettina."

The two girls inclined heads. Then they raised them to look at each other. The pink deepened in Bettina's cheeks and Astra felt a need for air. It was very hot in the small, cluttered room. The door of the stove stood open and an enormous wood fire was roaring halfway up the chimney. The windows were shut tight. They were not used to warm rooms. In North America rooms were often stifling, they had heard, from the central heating, and you weren't allowed to open windows.

"Please do sit down," said Frau Schneider.

The two families ranged themselves on opposite sides of the stove, Hugo making the middle point in the semicircle. Frau Schneider and Bettina poured coffee and passed around carrot cake and parsnip cake and rhubarb tart. The two women had been busy all morning.

"This is delicious," said Kristina, of the carrot cake, as soon as she'd taken a bite.

"Bettina made that," said her mother. "And the tart, too."

"That is also excellent," said Lukas, who was eating a large slice. All the pieces cut by Frau Schneider seemed huge to them, whose appetites had shrunk over the past four years. "I haven't tasted such good tart in a long time."

Bettina smiled, and she and Hugo exchanged looks. A sharp pain stabbed Astra's chest. She was not hungry but she struggled through a piece of the tart, declining further offers.

"It was very good, though," she said, giving up her plate.

Most of the conversing was done by the two fathers. The remainder of the company ate cake and drank coffee and glanced uneasily at one another. On the way there Kristina had said it was bound to be a rather awkward occasion, when the Schneiders knew that they hoped Hugo would come to Canada with them and the Petersons knew that the Schneiders hoped that Hugo would stay with them. When interests were so diametrically opposed it could not be a relaxed meeting. "Poor Hugo, he must feel yanked apart between us!"

After they'd eaten and drunk, Lukas suggested that the

young ones go for a walk and leave the elders to talk a little. Hugo led the way out.

They took a path through a wood that brought them out into a village. Hugo walked in the middle, turning from side to side to speak to each of the girls in turn. He told Astra about the people in the village. "That's where Bettina's best friend, Hilde, lives. They're very close, like you and Mara. And Doctor Braun used to live there. He was a good friend to me. He encouraged me to think of being a doctor." Astra nodded, though found it difficult to take in what he was saying. Too many other thoughts were swirling around inside her head. And also, she was thinking, a whole part of life that Hugo had lived had not contained her and never would mean anything to her. Until their flight from Latvia every significant event in their lives had been shared.

As they reached the top of the village she saw Hugo reach for Bettina's hand and link his fingers with hers. They turned in toward each other and smiled and for that moment forgot that she existed. I believe he really does love her, she thought dully.

Hugo did feel torn apart, pulled in one direction by his family and in the other by Bettina and the Schneiders, though neither party was deliberately trying to pull. Except for Astra who said openly and bluntly, "I can't go along with this nonsense of trying not to influence you, of leaving you to make up your own mind. I *want* you to come with us, Hugo, and I'm telling you so. I won't be able to bear it if you don't." The very idea that he might not burned like a ball of fire inside her, threatening to consume her.

He understood how she felt—he would have felt the same way himself had the positions been reversed. They had always understood each other, known what the other was thinking without having to put it into words. Their telepathy would bring them from separate rooms at the same instant with the same thoughts in their minds, their lips ready to frame the same words.

He wanted to go with his family, to make a new life with them in a new land. But he also wanted to stay with Bettina and make a life with her here in Germany.

He tramped many miles, across country, along the canal banks, and through the streets of Hamburg. He could not bear the containment of the Schneiders' kitchen and the troubled eyes of Bettina's mother, who followed his movements as if she expected that they might give a clue to his thoughts. He did not blame her for watching him anxiously. The happiness of her daughter was at stake—Hugo was well aware of that.

"It is a big decision," his father had said to him, when they'd had a long talk together, "and whatever you decide you are going to hurt some people—that you have to accept."

He had only one more day left in which to make up his mind. Tomorrow he had an appointment for a medical examination and X ray. If he passed he would be given a passage with his family. It was rumored that they were to sail in three days' time.

He said to Bettina, "If I were to go—and I am not saying that I will—but if I *were* to, I could send for you as soon as possible."

"How could I leave my mother and father? They need me. I am all they have whereas your parents have three children."

"They could come, too. Father could stand guarantor for them."

"My father would never pass the medical. And how could he earn money? Your father wouldn't be able to support us, nor could we allow him to. And could you see Mother leaving this house? She has lived here since her marriage."

Hugo resumed his perambulations. Inside the house, his brain ceased to function at all; outside, it began to operate again even if it came to no definite conclusion.

He ought to stay with the Schneiders, he owed it to them, they had saved his life. On the other hand, he ought to go with his family, his own flesh and blood, who had suffered so much in the last four years, who had lost their home, their country, and now, having found a son, stood to lose him again.

He was deeply fond of the Schneiders and he loved Bettina. But he also loved his family and felt attached to Astra as if by a cord. The one set of attachments did not rule out the other.

Bettina said that he could not expect to spend his whole life with his twin, it would not be healthy, and the cord would have to be cut sometime, just as a baby's cord is cut from its mother after birth. But the trouble was that he and Astra had been separated too soon: his life with her felt unfinished. A lot of unfinished business was left after wars, however—though knowing that did not make it easier to accept.

His mind continued to go around in circles. At times he thought his head would burst. The scar on his forehead began to throb and his eyes to hurt and he wore holes in the soles of his shoes.

In the end, it was Herr Schneider who helped him to make up his mind. He joined him on a walk through the wood. Hugo was reminded of the walk they had taken together after the war when he had returned from Leipzig. Herr Schneider was a calm, sensible man and Hugo had always found it helpful to talk to him.

"You have a terrible choice to make, Hugo, and I'm

deeply sorry for you, for the problem is not of your making. It's just fate! I think that you should do whatever it is that you most want to do, what your own heart dictates, and not allow all the ifs and ands and buts to get in the way, nor gratitude nor duty, either. We know you are grateful; your family knows you are a dutiful and a loving son."

The Petersons' sailing came through before the Jansons'. The families said their good-byes at the camp, making them as brief as possible—they had had enough good-byes in their lives not to want to linger over them. And these ones were particularly painful.

"We have been through so much together," said Olga as she and Kristina embraced.

"I know, Olga, but we'll all be together again soon, I'm sure we will. We'll see you in North America!"

Lukas and Paulis shook hands and clapped each other on the shoulder. There seemed no need to speak.

Tomas thumped Zigi on the back and said, "See you, Zig!" and then he ran, head down, into the bus that would transport them to Cuxhaven.

Astra and Mara kissed each other and did their best not to show their tears. They renewed their promises to write to each other.

"Every week!" said Astra, who felt as if she were going to choke. Mara was like a sister to her! "A long, long letter telling *everything*."

Mara nodded.

"Come on then, everyone," said Lukas, "the bus is waiting."

The bus was full of DPs on their way to the New World. They were quiet as it rolled away from the camp. Astra and Tomas waved out of the back window until Mara and Zigi had become tiny specks in the distance. And then they disappeared.

When they arrived on the dock, they found Hugo waiting by the gangway of their ship with Herr Schneider and Bettina. Frau Schneider had been too upset to come. Herr Schneider shook hands with the Petersons and wished them well in their new life, then he put his hands one on either side of Hugo's shoulders.

"Good luck, Hugo! We will think of you."

"And I you. I'll be back." Hugo swallowed. "Thank you," he started to say but Herr Schneider was already walking briskly away, toward the sheds.

"We'll go on board, Hugo," said Lukas. "Good-bye, Bettina, my dear." He gave her his hand. Kristina kissed her.

Astra put her arms around Bettina and hugged her before turning to follow the rest of her family up the swaying gangway.

"Good-bye," Bettina called after them. "*Gute Reise*!" A good journey!

The wail of the ship's horn filled the air. Hugo and Bettina joined hands and looked at each other.

"You'll write?" she said, although they had discussed it and made promises many times.

"Of course. We're still betrothed, aren't we?"

She nodded and raised her right hand. On the third finger she was wearing one of the amber rings that his mother had carried from Latvia. Kristina had given it to Hugo to give to her.

"And I'll come back next autumn, Betti, I promise."

The decision he had taken was a compromise: he would spend a year with his family in Canada, finish his education there, and try to make some money to start his medical training in Hamburg the following year.

"But you might like life in Canada better than here," said Bettina sadly. "If so, I would understand."

"I *will* come back, Betti—haven't I promised? It really is just *auf wiedersehn*." Till we meet again!

She reached up and kissed him. "I will never forget you, Hugo," she said and then she, too, ran for the shelter of the sheds. He watched her go.

The horn went again, sounding a note of urgency. He turned back to the ship. The deck rail was crowded with emigrants taking their last look at Europe. He saw Astra's face among them. She waved. He lifted his bags and went slowly up the gangway to join her.